Love, Life and Linguine

By Melissa Jacobs

LOVE, LIFE AND LINGUINE
LEXI JAMES AND THE COUNCIL OF GIRLFRIENDS

Love, Life and Linguine

Melissa Jacobs

AVON
TRADE

An Imprint of HarperCollins*Publishers*

HarperCollins books may be purchased for educational, business, or sales promo-
tional use. For information please write: Special Markets Department,
HarperCollins Publishers Inc., 10 East 53rd Street, New York, NY 10022.

FIRST EDITION

Interior text designed by Elizabeth M. Glover

Library of Congress Cataloging-in-Publication Data

Jacobs, Melissa.
    Love, life and linguine / by Melissa Jacobs.—1st ed.
       p. cm.
ISBN-13: 978-0-06-074405-2
ISBN-10: 0-06-074405-7 (acid-free paper)
1. Women in the advertising industry—Fiction. 2. Triangles (Interpersonal
relations)—Fiction. 3. Family-owned business enterprises—Fiction.
4. Restaurants—Marketing—Fiction. 5. Restaurateurs—Fiction. 6. New Jersey—
Fiction. I. Title.

PS3610.A35646L68 2006
813'.6—dc22   2005016565

06 07 08 09 10 JTC/RRD 10 9 8 7 6 5 4 3 2 1

Because I am still Daddy's little girl.

Acknowledgments

Marlene Jacobs Kaplan
My sweet mommy, who teaches me to savor life

Dave Jacobs
The prime rib of brothers

My Juicy Council of Girlfriends
Monica Duvall, Kammie Gormezano, Susanna Goihman

Spicy Selina McLemore
Who knew which ingredients to add—
and which to delete—
to make L3 a better book

Deliciously Divine Betsy Amster
One very smart cookie, who makes me a better writer

Michael Klein
For dishing his sweet and sour tales of the restaurant business

Acknowledgments

Christopher Williams
Creme de la creme of photographers,
for the Lady Marmalade _head shot_

My Secret Ingredient

And to everyone, everywhere,
who embraced by first baby,
Lexi James and the Council of Girlfriends.
Merci mucho!

◗━▭ Home

"Welcome home." The U.S. Customs agent smiles as she closes my blue passport.

Minutes later, a cab carries me away from Philadelphia International Airport toward the heart of the city. Ah, yes. I'm home.

Two weeks in Paris seemed like two months. It was a business trip. I had to go. But I was anxious to return. I'm starting a new chapter in my life. Before I left for Paris, I moved in with my boyfriend, Nick. Technically, my boxes moved into Nick's house. I didn't have time to unpack before I left.

I should have rescheduled the Paris trip. But when else could I have gone? Today is my last day with Dine International. Tomorrow I become the business manager of Il Ristorante, Nick's restaurant.

Not for the first time today, I look at my tote and read the business card placed behind the protective plastic. "Mimi Louis, Executive Restaurant Consultant, Dine International."

Mimi Louis isn't my real name. I was born Miriam Louis. I nicknamed myself Mimi when I was a toddler and couldn't pronounce my own name. The Louis? My grandfather left Russia a Luvizpharska and arrived in Brooklyn a Luvitz. My father left Brooklyn a Luvitz and arrived in South Jersey a Louis. What's in a family name?

My name might not be real, but my job is. Seven years. That's how long I've been at Dine International. I'm ready for a change. I'm ready to stop traveling. I'm ready to settle down and work on my relationship with Nick. We've been dating for three months, and I want Nick to be It.

I've paid my dating dues. I had the amuse bouche of boys in high school, the butlered hors d'oeuvres of Penn guys in college and the soup du jour men in my early twenties. When I was twenty-eight, I had what I thought was a main course relationship, but there were too many ingredients swirling around my life. My ambition, his ambition. My traveling, his traveling. My promotions, his promotions. We didn't make time for our relationship, let alone a future. After that breakup, I had a palate cleansing rebound in Florence with Gio the Italian wine maker. Now, at thirty, I'm ready for the entrée. The main course. Marriage.

Nick is ready for marriage, too. I know this. How? I know chefs.

Seduction by Risotto

Being a woman in the restaurant industry, I am used to being preyed upon by male chefs. But Nick? He's different. For starters, he's the most talented cook I've ever met.

Before Nick became Philadelphia's newest celebrity chef, he was the cook at a thirty-seat restaurant in South

Philadelphia. A date took me to Nick's for dinner. It was amazing. The food. Not the date. The next day, I told my bosses at Dine International that we should recruit Nick to be the chef at the new Italian restaurant we were already building on Avenue of the Arts. A month later, the deal was done.

Nick and I worked side by side to create the new restaurant. He flirted with me, and although I was hesitant to get involved with a client, my resolve crumbled when Nick invited me to his house for dinner. His passion for food ignited my passion for him. Nick cooked pan-seared salmon in white wine and herb sauce with julienned zucchini and yellow squash. And risotto. It was the risotto that did it. The textures of the rice and cream combined with the earthiness of the mushrooms. It was seduction by risotto. I couldn't resist Nick. I didn't.

Mustard Memories

"Where are you going, miss?" the cabdriver asks, jolting me away from Nickalicious memories. I have given him Center City as a destination, but it's time to get specific.

"One moment, please," I say. Am I going straight to the office or do I have time to stop at Nick's? There's no room in my head for my schedule. I am BlackBerry dependent. Reaching into my tote, my hand closes around a glass jar of mustard I bought in a shop near Musée Rodin. I collect mustard.

*   *   *

When I was a child, I would lie in bed at night, trying to stay awake until Dad got home from Café Louis, the dressed-up diner he owned in South Jersey. Dad's workaholism made precious any moments I had alone with him. If I could stay awake until Dad came home, I would tiptoe down the stairs so as not to wake Mom, who was usually asleep after a long day of housework, car pooling, and homework.

I adore my mother. She is, as Dad always said, a real looker. Mom has shoulder-length, gray blond hair and dark green eyes. Mom is thin, although she eats like a horse. I wish I had Mom's looks, and metabolism, but I have dark, wavy hair and milk chocolate eyes from my father's family.

As much as I love Mom, I always felt closer to Dad. I loved hanging out in the restaurant with him. I would greet the regulars and they would say, "There's Jay's little girl." On school nights when I couldn't be in the restaurant, I would try to wait up for Dad.

I'd turn on the kitchen lights and be waiting for Dad when he came through the door. "You should be in bed," he would say. It was the opening line of our routine.

I'd say my line. "I'm hungry, Daddy."

"No one should go to bed on an empty stomach," he'd answer.

Sandwiches were our late night snacks. Dad could make a sandwich from anything in the refrigerator. He was a leftover artist, but he never compromised on mustard. "Good mustard makes everything taste better," Dad would say. "Now, my Mimi, tell me about your day. What's the what?"

We continued this tradition through my childhood and adolescence, right up until I left for college. As I got older, it got easier to wait up for Dad, but harder to tell him about my life. He didn't want to hear about boys, but I always wanted to hear the daily goings on at Café Louis. First, though, came the making of the sandwich. Dad constantly reminded me about the mustard. "Good mustard makes all the difference," he said. "Are you listening, *bubbeleh*? Pay attention to the little things in life. Like mustard."

I can hear his voice. Booming, with the Yiddish lilt of his parents. He looked like Tevye from *Fiddler on the Roof*. The beard. The belly. Jay Louis is larger than life. Was. He died two years ago.

The Diva

"Where are you going?" the cabdriver asks again.

"Il Ristorante," I tell him. "On the Avenue of the Arts."

It's just after four o'clock. I have thirty minutes before my meeting. Just enough time for some smoochies.

You have time for more than that, the diva says. It's been two weeks. I have needs. Wants. Demands. Take Nick into his office and have at it. The diva groans.

Luckily, only I can hear her. Not that I'm embarrassed to talk to her. Men have been talking to their penises for eons. Why can't I talk to my diva?

◖═══╡ *The First Lady*

The cabbie pulls onto the Avenue of the Arts while I look at my face in my compact.

I need a WASAP. Waxing as soon as possible. With all the traveling I've done over the years, I should have had a waxer in every major city. The rest of me is presentable. Under my white trench coat, I'm wearing my flight suit. Black pencil skirt, white blouse, black pumps. The rest of my wardrobe is more colorful. I like pinks, lavenders, and soft greens. But in my flight suit, I can go from plane to meeting to dinner.

"Traffic," the cabdriver says as he gestures to the cars trying to merge onto Broad Street. When the boulevard twinkles with theater, music, and fine dining, I think of it as the Avenue of the Arts. When it is constipated with cars, I think of it as Broad Street. Same road. Different attitudes.

"I'll get out here," I tell the cabbie. It will be faster to walk the few blocks to Il Ristorante. The cabdriver pulls to the curb and takes my suitcase from his trunk.

"Come on, Olga," I tell my suitcase as I roll her down the street. If Olga could speak, she would no doubt complain. "Why are you hauling my kishkes all over town?" Yes, Olga the Suitcase would speak Yiddish. She was a gift from my father.

As Olga and I roll down Broad Street, a warm May breeze nuzzles my face and refreshes my spirit. Then I spy

Il Ristorante and smile at the dinner crowd forming. Should I have called first? Too late now. I'll surprise Nick.

"Welcome home, Mimi!" Gina the hostess says with delight. "Let me find Nick for you."

"You're busy," I tell Gina. Dinner starts in forty-five minutes, and everyone has something to do. "I'll find him."

Civilians are not allowed to roam unattended through a restaurant, but I am the First Lady of Il Ristorante. Nick is the front man, but I influenced everything from the decor to the menu. Then, it was my job. Now, it is my future.

As I walk through the dining room, my eyes evaluate every detail. The purple, gold, and green patterned banquettes. The burgundy and gold striped upholstery on the dark wood chairs. The marble bar enhanced by the enormous gilded mirror hanging behind it. Green plants sprouting from every corner. The decor is posh perfection.

Creating the menu was more difficult than designing the restaurant. At his South Philadelphia restaurant, Nick cooked amazing Italian-American food. His meatballs were legendary. The move uptown inspired Nick to fool around with cilantro and lemon grass. Dine International, which owns half of the restaurant, wanted Nick to stick to his roots and not reach beyond his means. Like a culinary Savonarola, I purged the menu of its artistic fusions and reinstated traditional Italian dishes. It worked. The restaurant is a hit.

"Nick?" I ask everyone as I make my way through the kitchen. They shake their heads and don't volunteer to help me find him. "Nick?" I keep going. This Marco Polo game is nothing new. Chefs don't stand still for long in their own restaurants.

Finally I hear Nick's voice and turn toward the dish room. There he is, explaining to the three dishwashers that he wants the silver flatware hand cleaned, not just tossed into the car wash, which is what we call the enormous industrial dishwasher.

"*Buon giorno*," I say from behind Nick.

Turning, Nick smiles. "Mimi."

"I'm home," I tell him.

Flatware crisis solved, Nick leads me into his office and shuts the door. Nick's office is just as horrid as every other chef's office. Windowless and airless, it's the size of a coat closet. Wedged into the office is a wood veneer desk that looks like it was trash picked. Half of the desk is consumed by a fax machine that overflows with notices from vendors announcing the daily or weekly specials. The other half of the desk is dedicated to a computer, the main server for the restaurant's ordering and inventory network. Since the computer is the brain of the entire restaurant, you would think it would be cared for and protected. Nope. I have cleaned grill grease, olive oil, and tomato sauce from the monitor. From the keyboard I have emptied snipped parsley leaves, dried citrus pith, and salt.

Nick's street clothes hang on the back of the door while his dirty chef pants and chef coats lie in a heap on the floor, emitting the odor of sweat, herbs, and fried food. An extra pair of kitchen clogs wait on a shelf. Unopened mail forms a carpet, cookbooks are stacked in the corners, a half-empty Rolodex yawns on the desk, and an open drawer reveals socks, deodorant, Altoids, and hair goop, which Nick uses to tame his brown, wavy locks. I have often thought that chefs' offices are like the inside of boys' lockers.

Nick sits on his office chair and I straddle him. "I missed you," I whisper and kiss him, gently opening his lips with my tongue. Pesto is what he tastes like, which means his staff has made a fresh batch and Nick's been sampling it all morning to make sure it is up to his standards. I never know how Nick's mouth will taste. It's like an Everlasting Gobstopper.

The diva smiles.

There's a knock at the door. "What?" Nick says.

"We have the specials ready," sous chef Jimmy reports. Nick serves and explains the specials to the waiters so they can accurately describe them, i.e., sell them, to customers. I ask my chefs to do this so waiters don't have to invent descriptions of dishes.

"I have to go," Nick says. He stands, but I bend my legs around his waist. Nick is more than six feet tall, and quite strong. "I really have to go," Nick says. He gives me a last kiss as I plant my feet on the ground.

"I'm going to leave Olga here," I tell Nick. "Will you take her home?"

"Chef!" someone hollers.

Nick nods and strides out the door like a general about to face his army.

* * *

9

I have my own army to face, although I'm doing a retreat, not an advance. I am reporting on my Parisian trip, and handing the client off to Claire McKenzie, my replacement.

"In summary, the opening was a success," I tell the group of people assembled around Dine International's conference table at this late meeting. "Brasserie Jardin's growing pains are the same as any other restaurant. Chef Galieu's food cost average was ridiculous, until I reminded him that he's playing with DI money. The labor cost is double what it should be, but I expect Chef to fire half his kitchen staff before the end of the month. The wine list needs to be expanded once Chef is convinced that Burgundy isn't the only region in France which makes excellent wines."

My colleagues laugh. To Claire, I say, "You need to be tough with this chef. You need to know everything that goes on in that restaurant. When he cooks, when he doesn't cook, who he hires, who he fires, how much he drinks, who he screws and how much his wife knows. DI's made an investment in this man. Remind him of that. Understand?"

Claire blinks at me. "Okay," she says.

"Mimi," says Peter Exter, president of DI. "Your stilettos will be hard to fill."

My farewell dinner takes place in Dine International's office, which is a renovated brownstone complete with kitchen and dining room. We have to audition chefs, so it makes sense to have our own facilities. What Peter has arranged is a dinner featuring dishes from the four restaurants I opened this year in Philadelphia. Chicken satay with peanut sauce from Kai's Thai, bouillabaisse from Brasserie X, paella from Blanco, and a huge dessert tray from Le Sucre. After dessert, my boss brings out the champagne. Veuve Clicquot. My favorite. "By the way," my boss says, "we didn't get food from Nick's because you'll be eating that for the rest of your life."

"God I hope so," I say. "Thank you, Peter, for this great party. DI has been my home and you all have been my family. Which is why I feel comfortable saying that, if you really love me, you'll come into Il Ristorante and spend mondo money."

Peter raises his glass. "Good luck, Mimi. *Bonne chance, salud, and santé.*"

By ten o'clock, the party is over. I'm only a few blocks from Il Ristorante. Might as well haul my jet-lagged tush over there and wait for Nick. What with all the crap in his office, Nick will probably forget about my suitcase.

When I get to the restaurant, the last diners are drinking six-dollar espresso concoctions. Smiling at the servers doing their closing side work, I walk through the kitchen and see the cooks cleaning their stations. When I get to Nick's office, I knock on the door, but there is no answer. Has Nick left for the night? I have to get Olga. Using my key, I swing open the office door.

Nick stands with his chef pants around his knees. A young woman in a waitressing outfit kneels on the floor in front of him. At the sight of me, the girl's jaw drops and I see that her tongue is pierced. That, for some reason, is the ultimate insult. I may have more money, more career success, and more intelligence than that girl. But she has a pierced tongue, and I don't.

◼︎◼︎◻ *Olga, the Diva, and Me*

Happy? I ask the diva as we stride up Walnut Street toward Rittenhouse Square.

Of course I'm not happy, the diva says. Listen, darling . . .

I've listened to you quite enough. If I'd gone straight to my office from the airport, I wouldn't have left Olga at the restaurant. If I hadn't gone back to the restaurant to get Olga, I wouldn't have walked in on . . . that.

It's better that you know, the diva says.

I don't want to know, I say.

Oy, Olga says.

We reach Rittenhouse Square. I sit on a park bench and pull Olga next to me.

I can't believe Nick did that, I say. And in front of Olga.

I saw the whole thing, Olga says.

Tell me what happened, I say.

You know what happened, the diva says. And you know why it happened.

We should go to Madeline's, Olga says.

If I hadn't listened to you, I tell the diva, I never would've dated Nick.

The diva is silenced.

■—🔱 *Breakup Cake*

"Oh, and I didn't even tell you the funny part," I say to Madeline.

There is no funny part, but Madeline is my best friend and will listen to whatever I have to say. She also has to listen because I am shouting. In her apartment.

"What's the funny part?" Madeline asks calmly from her couch.

"I hired that waitress."

Madeline sighs. "Chefs make horrible boyfriends and girlfriends."

"You're a chef."

"That's how I know," Madeline says. "But I'm a pastry chef. Different species."

Madeline is the executive pastry chef at Tiers, the homonymly unfortunate name of Philadelphia's top wedding cake shop. Madeline is short and thin but muscular, with dyed blond hair and dramatic black eyebrows. She got through culinary school and pastry apprenticeships not because she is pretty, but because she is talented and hardworking. Yes, Madeline is a tough cookie.

"Nick is evil," she states. Things are simple in Madeline's chocolate and vanilla world.

"I shouldn't have traveled so much. I should've been there for him."

"Don't blame yourself," Madeline says. "Blame him.

Blame the girl. She's a traitor." Madeline knows about tarts of all kinds.

"Do you think it was just that once?" I ask quietly. "Just her?"

"I don't know." Madeline's voice has an edge to it. She either doesn't think it a one-time incident, or she doesn't care.

Madeline rises from her couch and goes to her refrigerator. She returns with two forks and a plate, on which sits a piece of hot pink cake.

"What in the Julia Child is that?" I ask.

"One of my brides wanted a fuschia wedding cake. I did a small test cake. She changed her mind." Madeline hands me a forkful. "But it tastes good."

"I just broke up with my boyfriend and you're feeding me wedding cake?" I say.

Madeline considers this while she chews. "Think of it as breakup cake."

I accept that, and the forkful of cake. My cell rings. Madeline looks at the caller ID. "It's Nick."

"I don't want to talk to him. Do you think he's calling to apologize?"

Madeline shrugs. Again, she doesn't know and doesn't care. Madeline says, "You should sleep. You'll think more clearly in the morning. The guest room is yours for as long as you want it. My home is your home. Okay?"

"Okay. Thanks, Maddie."

In an awkward but touching gesture, Madeline leans toward me. She kisses the top of my head. Her exterior is tough, but Madeline has a soft, chewy center.

◼━◻ *Nicco*

The ringing of a phone wakes me. Eyes closed, I reach toward the nightstand and the phone. "Hello," I mumble into my cell.

"Did I wake you?" Nick asks. "It's two o'clock in the afternoon."

"Whatever," I mumble.

"Do you want to talk?" Nick asks. Then, "Hold on, Mimi." Nick shouts, "Jimmy! The fish guy is here with the late delivery. Can you go sign for it?" I hear the bustle of the restaurant. "Okay," Nick says. "I'm back."

"Why don't you call me when you're not at the restaurant?"

"It's Friday," Nick says. "The reservation book is filled. I can't leave. But I want to talk about this now, before it gets worse."

"Worse?"

"Mimi, I don't want you to blow this out of proportion."

"Well, Nick, I don't think you should be using the word 'blow.' "

Nick exhales into the phone. "Where are you?"

"Madeline's."

"Great," Nick says. "She'll probably jump me in an alley and stab me with a candy thermometer."

That makes me laugh. Nick laughs, too. Then he says, "Will you please come to the restaurant? We can talk out front."

* * *

Should I forgive him? As I cab toward Il Ristorante, I try to think clearly. He'll apologize. He'll ask for another chance. Can we get past this? Other couples have survived infidelity. Maybe it will strengthen our relationship. But if I forgive him too easily, I'll appear desperate. I need to be strong.

As the cab pulls up to the restaurant, I see Nick talking to diners who are entering the restaurant. "Thanks," he calls to them as they go inside and I get out of the cab. "I'm going to cook your dinner specially!"

Turning to me, Nick says, "They saw me on television. I was on two morning shows while you were gone. And the *Daily News* did a big story with my picture in it. All of a sudden, people know who I am. They want to talk to me and shake my hand. I'm, like, a big shot."

"Hey, Nick," I say. "There's a valet if you want to park your ego."

"Nicco," he says.

"Pardon?"

"Call me Nicco from now on. It sounds more Italian than Nick."

"I could call you a few other names. Pick a language."

"Very funny," Nick says. He puts his hands in the pockets of his black chef pants. "Listen, Mimi, I'm sorry you walked in on . . . that."

"Fellatio interruptus. Sounds like a pasta dish."

"You don't know what's been going on here. I'm under a lot of pressure. It's the three-month mark. Restaurant critics are starting to come in for reviews. Dine International is looking over my shoulder. The staff complains about everything. I'm stressed out."

This conversation is supposed to be about me and my righteous indignation. "Is that what you were doing with tongue ring girl? Relieving stress?"

"Listen," Nick says. "I hope we can be friends."

"Friends?" I ask. This conversation is getting off course. Where's the grovel?

Nick holds up his hands. "While you were away, I realized that we don't want the same things. You want a husband, children, and a house in the suburbs. You've had a successful career and now you're ready to settle down. But I'm just starting to make it big. I want to enjoy it. Being the chef of a restaurant is like being a rock star."

"So, what? It's sex, drugs, and linguine?"

Nick glares at me.

"Anyway, you're not a rock star. Dine International wanted you for your cooking skills, not your guitar work. Don't forget that."

Nick shakes his head. "That right there is why this relationship isn't working. You can't separate your work from your personal life. You're not supposed to manage me like I'm a client. You're supposed to be my girlfriend."

"Girlfriends aren't supportive?" I say.

"There's a difference between being supportive and being controlling."

"I don't want to control you. I want you to benefit from my expertise. Since when is me being a restaurant consultant a bad thing?"

"It's not just the job," Nick says. "It's your whole life.

You have a great career. You're a world traveler. You have your own apartment. Your own stock portfolio. Your own everything. You don't need me for anything."

I stare at Nick's black kitchen clogs and absorb his words. "So you would be more secure if I were more insecure?"

Nick leans against the brick wall and runs his hand through his hair. He knows he can't out-logic me. I win the witty repartee contest. Fat lot of good it'll do me.

Nick says, "You think you're so smart, Mimi, but you don't know everything."

"Is that right?"

"Yeah, it is. You think men want to feel inferior? That we want to be pressured? Domesticated? You know a lot, Mimi. But you don't know what men want."

"Okay. Fine. I didn't mean to pressure you. I mean, Nick, I just . . ."

"Nicco," he says without looking at me.

 em:==⊏ *Mathematics*

"Ouch." Madeline winces.

"Nick turned all of my attributes into faults," I say.

"He's wrong," Madeline says. She's perched on the arm of her couch, all of her muscles taut and ready to spring into action. But there's nothing she can do. What's done is done.

"Maybe Nick's right," I say, staring at a spot on the wall. "Maybe I am too independent. But I spent my twenties working so I could spend my thirties raising a family. I thought that's what I was supposed to do. I thought I had time. I thought I'd meet someone, eventually. Later. But it is later. And I'm alone. And old."

"You're not old," Madeline says.

"Do the math, Maddie. I'm thirty. Let's say I meet someone tomorrow. To date, get engaged, and plan a wedding would take a year, and that's moving at lightning speed. I'd be thirty-one, at least. Say we spend a year being newlyweds, fixing up the house, whatever. Then I try to get pregnant. There's no guaranteeing that I'll get pregnant right away. So, allow a year to get and be pregnant. That means I'll have my first child when I'm thirty-three. Then I have to recover, nurse, and try to get pregnant again. Another year passes. Then I spend another year pregnant. That means I'll have my second child when I'm thirty-five. Thirty-five, Maddie. And that's assuming I meet someone tomorrow. Which I won't. Not tomorrow. Not ever."

"Mimi, lots of women today don't even start families until after thirty-five. You are a strong, successful, intelligent woman. Nick's not man enough to handle you. He doesn't know what all men want."

"Do men want women like me?"

"Who cares what men want?" Madeline says. "We know what we want. That's all that matters."

But Madeline is wrong. I look at her through glassy eyes.

"Yell," Madeline says. "Scream. Let it out. Hit something. Not me. Something else. You'll feel better."

Strong, successful, and intelligent I may be. But right

this minute, there's only one thing that will make me feel better.

I want my mommy.

Sally

I schlep Olga four blocks to my garage, where sits my car. It's a 1966 Mustang GT convertible. Beige leather interior, white body with black LeMans stripes and a black power top. Her name is Sally. She belonged to Dad, but now she's mine. Stripping the car of her tarp, I whisper, "Hello, girlfriend."

Home

To get to Mom, I have to get to Lenape Hill, New Jersey. It's a half-hour drive from Philadelphia. When I turn Sally onto the Benjamin Franklin Bridge, I look out at the dark waters of the Delaware River and try to remember the last time I went home.

Well, it's not exactly home. Home will always be the house in which I grew up, which is in Westfield, New Jersey. It's the same distance from Philadelphia, but in the opposite direction of where Mom now lives. A few months ago, Mom sold our Westfield house and bought a townhouse in a development called The Garden. With Dad gone, Mom said she didn't need a whole house. I have visited The Garden townhouse twice. It's nice. The thing is this: Mom's new house is Mom's house. Not Mom and Dad's house.

Sally and I cruise down the Ben Bridge and merge onto Admiral Wilson Boulevard. The sign on my right says, "Welcome to New Jersey."

I hold back my tears as if I'm holding my bladder and looking for a rest stop. We're almost there, I tell myself. Hold it in.

Up and over a ramp and onto another highway. This one is Route 108. It carries me past full-service gas stations, dollar stores, and more Dunkin' Donuts than seems necessary. Lonestar Steakhouse, Outback Steakhouse, Subway, Quizno's, TGI Friday's, Houlihan's, Pizzeria Uno, Pizza Hut. Only yesterday I was sipping a café crème on Boulevard Saint Germain.

When I get to Kean Road, I turn left and drive quickly away from the highway to strip mall hell. Then comes heaven, or at least purgatory. Trees. Woods. A farm. And hey, a farmstand. Oh, Jersey. My schizophrenic state.

Finally I see the giant sign for The Garden, Mom's development.

The Garden's neat townhouses sit side by side, ten to a street. The houses have identical gray siding. The color of the trim varies. Cranberry red, spinach green, dark peach. Mom lives on Tomato Road and when I turn onto it, I breathe easier.

"Come on, Olga." I wheel her to Mom's front door and realize that I don't have a key to Mom's townhouse. Why would I? I don't live within shouting distance like my brother.

It feels weird to ring the doorbell at my mother's house. But I do, and hear the chimes. Quickly, I smooth my frantic hair and try to wipe away the black mascara that leaked onto my cheeks. It's no use. I'm a mess. Lace curtains on the door separate and a pair of green eyes look at me. The door opens. "Hello, gorgeous," Mom says.

I start to cry.

◼━◁ *Bobbi Louis*

"Oh, honey!" Mom pulls me into her house. I leave Olga by the door and let Mom lead me to her taupe couch.

"What happened?" Mom says as she puts her arms around me.

I tell Mom my tale of woe. Rather, I start to tell her. The phone rings, interrupting me. "Let me get that," Mom says. But the phone gets her. Mom chatters away to someone named Helen.

Leaning out of the kitchen, Mom says, "I'll be off in a minute."

No hurry. I'll still be a mess when she gets off the phone.

While Mom continues her conversation, I look around the living room. Mom's done quite a bit of decorating since last I was here. The room is done in soft, feminine colors. Pale peach walls, beige carpeting, glass and chrome etagere, egg white couches, champagne and peach pillows. A vase of white tulips sits on the blond wood coffee table. Nice. Different from Westfield. But nice.

"Sorry," Mom apologizes when she comes back to the couch. "That was Helen."

"Okay," I say, having no idea who Helen is. "Did you have plans for tonight?" It didn't occur to me that she would.

Mom waves her hands, which I see are French manicured. That, too, is different. Dad liked his woman to wear red nail polish. "Helen and I are taking a sculpture class. She can go without me."

"You sculpt?" Who is this woman?

"I'm not going anywhere," Mom says firmly. "Tell me the rest of the story."

⬤▬◀ *Lipstick Theory*

When I finish describing Nick's philandering, Mom looks angry. She says, "I'm going to call his mother."

I laugh.

"I'm serious," Mom says. "I called Stevie Klein's mother when he broke up with you right before the winter dance."

"That was in eighth grade, Mom."

"Stevie got grounded for a month for being a schmuck."

"I don't think Nick's mother is going to ground him," I say. "But I appreciate the sentiment, Mom."

"Nobody makes my little girl cry," Mom says fiercely. "Although . . ."

"What?"

"Well, Mimi, you did rush into the relationship with Nick. You dated him for, what? Three months? You should've gotten to know him better before you quit your job and gave up your apartment."

"Mom," I say, wounded.

"What? You came to me for help. I'm helping."

"I didn't come to you for help. I came to you for comfort. Can't you make me chicken soup or something?"

"I'm all out of chicken soup," Mom says, "but I can give you a bowl of logic."

What does Mom's logic look like? Dad was the logic chef. From Mom, I only ordered comfort. No matter. I say, "It's too soon for logic. First comes moping. Logic comes later."

"You can mope as long as you want. And you can stay here as long as you want. You want your mommy? You got her."

"Thanks, Mom." Really? I want my dad.

"You know, Mimi, I do feel a maternal obligation to impart some wisdom."

I groan. "Go ahead."

"You thought Nick was the love of your life after your first date. From now on, you should go slower. Shop."

"Shop?"

"Sure," Mom says. "That's what dating is. Shopping for a partner. You don't buy the first lipstick you try on in the store, do you? You try on different lipsticks and see if they suit you. Same thing with dating."

"Maybe you're right," I say.

"Of course I'm right. Find the right lipstick. Find the right man."

I smile at Mom. "Lipstick theory for dating. Like chaos theory, only simpler."

Mom smiles back at me. "You're going to be okay, Mimi."

"Yeah." Exhaling, I lean against Mom. Which takes some doing, because I am considerably taller than she is. Arranging myself on the couch, I lie down and put my head in Mom's lap. She runs her hand through my hair.

"Mom, you know what really bothers me? Nick said that I don't know what men want."

Mom sighs. "Neither do they, baby. Neither do they."

◼▭◖ Allison Louis

The next morning, laughter wakes me. Padding barefoot into the kitchen, I see Mom sitting at the kitchen table with Allison Louis. My sister-in-law.

Allison looks perfect. She is perfect. I want to be Allison when I grow up.

Tiny and trim with highlighted blond hair, Allison is always wearing the right makeup, the right clothes, the right attitude. And why shouldn't she have the right attitude? Allison Louis is twenty-eight and she has a loving husband and three wonderful kids. Sarah is eight. Twins Gideon and Ezra are four.

"Good morning," Allison says in her musical voice.

"Good morning, honey," Mom says.

"Morning." I'm not ready to decide if it's good or not.

Mom says, "Ally and I usually have our breakfast club at her house, but I wanted to be here when you woke up. How do you feel, Mimi?"

"Fine. You have a breakfast club?"

Mom nods. "We have breakfast together twice a week. It was Ally's idea."

Mom and Allison smile at each other. I feel like the in-law.

Sisters-in-Law, Part One

Allison Greene met my brother at Penn. Jeremy was getting his MBA at Wharton. Allison was in Wharton undergrad.

I was in my first year of working for Dine International when Jeremy arranged for Allison to meet our family over brunch at the White Dog Café near Wharton. At the end of the meal, Allison went to the bathroom. Looking seriously at me, Dad, and Mom, Jeremy asked, "Do you like her?"

We nodded.

"Good," he said. "Because we're getting married."

"Married?" I blurted.

"Why?" Mom asked.

"What we mean," Dad said calmly, "is why are you getting married so soon?"

"Ally's pregnant," Jeremy answered. "I love her and she loves me. It'll be okay."

But we knew, the three of us, that this was not the life Jeremy had planned for himself. "Are you still going to Los Angeles?" I asked. He had been offered a mondo job at an accounting firm there.

Jeremy shook his head. "It's too far from Ally's parents. They live in New York. Although they are moving to Florida soon. Still, we're going to stay on the East Coast. I've had several job offers in Philadelphia. We'll buy a house in this area and stay close to home." Jeremy smiled at Mom and Dad. They smiled back. Everybody smiled at everybody, making the best of the situation.

"Here she comes," Jeremy said.

Allison came back from the bathroom, walking hesitantly toward our table, trying to discern the status of the conversation.

My father stood and folded Allison in his arms. "Welcome to the family."

Five months later, Sarah was born. Jeremy finished at Wharton, but Allison didn't. Jeremy became an MBA. Allison became a MOM.

Although she's been a Louis for eight years, I don't know Allison very well. She came into the family as I was leaving. To work, to travel, to boyfriend. Of course, we've seen each other at holidays and birthdays—the ones I attend—but we haven't formed a relationship independent of the family. So my image of Allison is as my brother's wife. A job at which she excels. Jeremy adores Allison.

So does Mom, apparently. It looks like they've grown even closer now that Mom lives in Lenape Hill, which is nearer than Westfield to Allison's house. It's good that Allison has Mom and Mom has Allison. Where does that leave me? I don't know. I guess I have to find where I fit in this revised version of the family Louis.

◖▬◗ *Someone to Dance With*

"What were you laughing about?" I ask Allison and Mom.

"We were talking about the wedding last weekend." Allison uses the pearly pink polished nail of her pinky finger to brush blond hair out of her eyes.

"What wedding?" I ask.

"Cousin Lauren's," Mom says. "It was a fabulous party."

"Why wasn't I invited?" I ask.

"You were," Mom says. "You said you couldn't go because of your trip to Paris."

"Oh." When was the last time I saw Lauren, or any of my cousins? I missed the family seder in April. I was in Rome. The Chanukah party? I was in Dallas. Gee. Looks like I'll be having guilt for breakfast.

"Tell me about the wedding," I say.

"Lauren's dress was beautiful," Allison starts.

"The band was great," Mom says, "even though I didn't dance."

"Why not?" I ask as I turn to the coffeepot. "You love dancing."

"Your aunts and uncles dance with each other," Mom says. "I don't have someone to dance with."

Mom states that as fact, without self-pity. But the sadness of the statement brings tears to my heart. Standing in front of the coffeepot, I keep my back to Mom and Allison, so Mom doesn't see the emotion on my face.

Allison says, "You should start to date."

That makes me laugh. "It's too soon for me."

"Not you. Mom."

Turning, I look at Mom. "You want to date?"

Mom shrugs.

"She doesn't want to be alone for the rest of her life," Allison says.

"She's not alone. She has me and Jeremy and you and the kids."

"It's not the same," Allison insists. "A woman needs a man."

Allison and I look at Mom. Mom looks at the kitchen table. "It would be nice."

I am stunned. Why am I stunned? Do I want Mom to be alone? No. But, I didn't think she was alone. I can't imagine her with anyone but my father.

"Some of my friends have found dates from the personals in the *Jewish Exponent*," Mom says. "Helen has been dating someone she met on the Internet."

"We'll go on the Internet," Allison decides. "Lots of people do that."

Yeah. People who aren't my mother. Shouldn't she, like, knit?

Mom looks at me. "What do you think, Mimi?"

Allison raises her eyebrows, willing me to be supportive. So now I have to be supportive. I can't be the bad daughter.

"If you want to date," I say, "then I think you should."

Mom smiles. "Really?"

No. "Yes."

Allison looks at her watch. "I have time. Let's go on the Internet now and look at websites. The three of us can do it together."

"Helen and I are going to a lecture and lunch at the JCC," Mom says. "But I don't have to leave for a while."

Help Mom troll the Internet for lovers? I'd rather not. "I have things to do."

"It's okay," Mom says to Allison. "Mimi's been through a rough few days."

I accept my pardon. Allison takes Mom's hand and the two of them leave the kitchen and go into the den. I hear them turn on the computer. They laugh. I decide to shower, and wash away the scent of despair.

◼━◀ *Bobbi's Ideal Mate*

After Allison leaves to collect the twins, Mom asks me to help her fill out her profile on an Internet site for singles over fifty. I can't think of a logical reason not to. Pulling up the dating site's profile screen, I start to fill in Mom's information. "Age?" I ask.

"You know how old I am," she says.

"Maybe we should skew downward. You look a lot younger than sixty. You could easily pass for fifty-five."

"Yeah," Mom says. "Let's start my dating life by lying."

"Fine." I type "60" into the age box. We finish the rest of the vital statistics.

Reading from the website, I say, "Name some characteristics and hobbies your ideal mate should have."

Mom thinks. "Someone who wants to travel."

"Dad never traveled."

"Intelligent," Mom continues. "Well read. Love of the performing arts."

I laugh. "Dad didn't like to go to plays or concerts."

"I know."

From the screen, I read, "What well-known person would be your ideal mate?"

Mom thinks for a moment. "Billy Crystal."

I turn around to look at her. "Billy Crystal?"

"Yes. He's Jewish. Funny. Smart. I don't know how old he is but he looks like he's in my generation. He's very witty at the Oscars. Helen and I went to see his one-man show on Broadway. Brilliant."

Turning back to the computer, I hit send and watch the screen as the information transmits. Then I realize that Mom's ideal mate is nothing like Dad. Why not?

Mom leaves for her lecture and lunch. I stand in the kitchen and I feel alone. I need to be somewhere I feel safe, and that place is not here, in Mom's new house with Mom's new life. Where can I go? Well, there is one place.

●━━◁ *Home*

Twenty minutes later, I sit in my car staring at Café Louis.

Although I haven't seen her for almost two years, Café

Melissa Jacobs

Louis looks the same. But worse. Her burgundy paint is peeling like chipped nail polish. Butterscotch-colored roof tiles are turning black at their roots. Crowning the restaurant is her once glittering tiara, a painted sign that reads "Café Louis." She looks like what she is. A relic. A discarded remnant of an era when independent and family-run restaurants dominated this area of New Jersey. The party is over; it's moved down the street to Red Lobster. But no one has told Café Louis. She wears lipstick and stockings and waits by the door, wondering when her guests will arrive.

And yet, I love her. Café Louis is part of me. Part of my family.

The restaurant business is hereditary, Dad said. As far as family legacies go, it's not so bad.

Café Louis is a descendant of Luvitz's Deli in Brooklyn, where my father learned the restaurant business at the nudging elbow of his father. Just as my father left the borscht-colored shadow of Luvitz's Deli, so did I leave the cheese fry–scented atmosphere of Café Louis. I ascended to the white-linen stratosphere of fine dining. But now I've come crashing back to the beginning, back to where I was taught to waitress and to cook, back to the place I got hooked on the restaurant world.

Sitting in Sally, I close my eyes and see my younger self, tripping on good tips, dancing with the cooks as we tried to keep up with the dinner rush. Drinking the camaraderie of the waiters.

And then, I turned the party into work. I took my waitressing smile to the board room and left the short, black

32

aprons to the younger, pierced girls. I lost my mise en place in the world. But I can get it back.

The glass door creaks as I open it and walk into the restaurant. It's midmorning. The waiters have yet to arrive. The house is empty. Slowly, I walk the length of the chrome counter, running my hand along the red leatherette and chrome stools. Behind the counter are soda fountains, a metal vat for iced tea, and display cases holding pies, cakes, and giant cookies. The dining area is lined with booths and filled in with tables of four. Everything is just as Daddy left it.

"Well, now." A voice comes from behind me. "Look who's come home."

⬛━━🍴 *Grammy Love*

Behind me stands Althea Jefferson, affectionately known as Grammy Jeff. She is a tall, round, black woman and she has been in charge of the lunch shift since I was a child.

Grammy Jeff folds me into her thick arms. "Honey, it's good to see you," she says in her North Carolina–flavored voice. "What brings you here?"

"You. I came to see you." Maybe that's true. Grammy Jeff was a source of comfort for all of the adolescent turmoil I couldn't tell my parents. Mostly boyfriend stuff. There was nothing I couldn't tell Grammy Jeff. She has lived through it all.

Grammy Jeff holds me away from her body. "You supposed to be at your fancy job, traveling around the world and such. Something bad must have happened. I'm guessing it has to do with a man. Am I right?"

"You're always right."

"Mmm-hmm." Grammy takes my hand. "Come on, then. I got to get ready for lunch, but I got time to make you something good to eat. You can tell me all about it."

Grammy Jeff's macaroni and cheese is a miracle to behold. I like watching Grammy cook the dish almost as much as I like eating it. Sitting on a stool next to the metal table, I watch Grammy pull a pasta pot, a double boiler, and a casserole dish from the storage area. When she has water on to boil and the cheddar melting, Grammy turns her attention to me. "Tell me what happened, baby girl."

By the time I finish the story, Grammy has cooked the macaroni and melted the cheddar. To the cheese, Grammy adds milk, eggs, butter, salt, and pepper. She puts the noodles into a casserole dish and drowns them in the sauce. Grammy puts the dish into the oven, then turns to me and says, "Let me tell you a story."

While the macaroni and cheese bubbles in the oven, Grammy tells me a story. She speaks in biblical parables. A devout Christian, Grammy has a biblical psalm, proverb, or parable for each of life's situations. Her voice is deep and it rises and falls in a beautiful rhythm. Now, Grammy says, "The lips of a forbidden woman drip honey. Her mouth is smoother than oil. But in the end, she is as bitter as wormwood, sharp as a two-edged sword. Proverbs, five," Grammy finishes. "Praise the Lord."

"Amen, Grammy," I readily acknowledge.

As Grammy places the casserole dish of macaroni and cheese on the metal utility table, the kitchen's back door slams. In walks a six-foot-five, thin man in his thirties wearing khakis and a Sean John T-shirt. This is Grammy's grandson, Nelson Jefferson.

"Good morning, my Jewish queen," he says.

"Good morning, my African prince," I reply.

Nelson doesn't ask what I'm doing at Café Louis. He doesn't ask a lot of questions. We've known each other since we were children, but we come from very different backgrounds and we've learned that it's best not to be nosy. Nelson is a good person who got dealt a bad hand in the form of his mother, Grammy's daughter, who had him when she was fourteen. Grammy raised Nelson after his mother left for parts unknown. He's helped Grammy in the kitchen for most of his life, and as he puts on a white chef coat, I realize that he's now a bona fide employee of Café Louis.

As if to answer my unasked question, Grammy says, "Nellie works the grill and the Fry-o-later during lunch."

"One person can handle the lunch crowd?" I ask.

"It's not so much of a crowd anymore," Grammy says.

Business is slow? That's news.

"Anyhow," Grammy says, "I do all the cold stuff ahead of time. Tuna salad, chicken salad, seafood salad, macaroni salad, potato salad. You know I make the best potato salad in New Jersey."

"Yes, ma'am," I say. But this a lot of work for one woman, especially one pushing sixty-five. Jumping off my stool, I say, "Let me help, Grammy. Where are the recipes?"

Grammy tsks. "Honey, I don't have recipes. I cook from my heart."

I laugh. "You don't want anyone to know your secret ingredient?"

"I'll tell you my secret ingredient," Grammy says. "Love."

When the first lunch order comes in, Grammy kicks me out of the kitchen. "Me and Nellie got a system," she says when I volunteer to help.

I walk into the hundred-seat dining room and see that only four waiters are working lunch. I guess business is really slow.

But the people who are eating here have been eating here for decades. Mrs. and Mr. Byrem. Dave Arthur and his firefighter buddies. Rabbi and Mrs. Levine. Mrs. Leopold, who leads a brigade of community volunteers. The Riesenbachs from down the road. Maury Levy. Marlene Kaplan and her daughter, whose name I can't remember. But they remember my name.

◼▬◗ *Restaurant Diva*

What exactly is the status of Café Louis? Getting my Nancy Drew on, I go to the downstairs office to sleuth for clues. Although it feels like I'm spying on my brother, I'm not really doing anything untoward. I own half of Café

Louis and I have the right—nay, the responsibility!—to check on Jeremy's management of the restaurant. After all, I am a restaurant consultant. So? Consult.

The office is the same mess it was when Dad was alive. The four-walled room is lined with wood bookshelves, most of which groan under the weight of piles of paper. Receipts, recipes, reviews. In the corner, an ancient, black-and-white TV spreads its antennae. On the wood veneer desk sits a beige telephone sprinkled with food particles. I sit in Dad's chair, a creaky metal contraption with torn leatherette cushioning.

Every man needs a throne, Dad said.

Other than the phone, the desktop is empty. No papers, no files, no computer. Dad mistrusted computers. So where is the paperwork? Opening drawers, I see decades of detritus. Pencil stubs, carbon copies of bank deposits, my fifth grade school photo, a repository of rubber bands, a postcard with "Greetings from Asbury Park" on the front. Turning the postcard, I read its message. "To, All my love, B." There's a lipsticked kiss next to the letter B. How cute are my parents?

In the bottom drawer of the desk, I find an expandable file folder with neatly marked tabs. It is so logical and neat that I assume the file folder is the work of my brother, not my father. Sure enough, the monthly pouches hold the information I want: paperclipped purveyor forms, stapled piles of credit card slips and bank deposits, and rubber-banded ordering slips decorated with the handwriting of waiters.

I organize the information, stacking piles of evidence

that can tell me the story of at least three months of business at Café Louis.

One number that's not here is liquor sales. Café Louis is a BYOB. Like many other restaurant owners, Dad never wanted to deal with New Jersey liquor laws. Had he purchased a liquor license in the seventies, subsequent liquor sales would've made back that money a hundred times over. Oh, well.

By late afternoon, I have formed a working theory about Café Louis. Check averages can be increased by making the menu à la carte to encourage customers to order more food instead of including soup, salad, and two sides with each entree. Food costs need to be lowered by finding more affordable purveyors. I can make this happen. I am a restaurant diva. Right? Of course, right.

Café Louis needs me. I need her. As far as codependencies go, it's not so bad.

Café Louis

Soup $3
Matzo Ball Soup   French Onion   Manhattan Clam Chowder   Soup du Jour

Salads $5
Tossed   Greek   Caesar
Cup of Soup and Salad $6.50   Cup of Soup and Half a Sandwich $8

Sandwiches
served with lettuce, tomato, pickle, and chips.
White, rye, pumpernickel, wheat, or Kaiser roll.
Grilled Cheese $5   Chicken Salad $6   Corned Beef $7   Jeremy's Club $8
Tuna/Egg Salad $5   Chicken Parm $6   Roast Beef $7   Meatball $8

Cold Platters $9
served with lettuce, tomato, onion, cole slaw, and the best potato salad in New Jersey
Chicken Salad   Tuna Salad   Egg Salad   Whitefish

Entrees
served with bread and butter, choice of soup or tossed salad, and two sides
Lasagna $10   10 oz. Sirloin Steak $13
Chicken Parmigiana $13   Spaghetti with Meatballs $10
My Wife's Meatloaf $13   Chicken Marsala $13
Fettuccine Alfredo $9   Brisket $13
Chicken Cordon Bleu $14   Broiled Scallops $14
Broiled Flounder $14   Shrimp Scampi $15

Sides
choice of two with entree, or $3 each
Mashed potatoes, baked potato, French fries, creamed spinach, rice pilaf

For Children $5
PB&J   Hot dog   Spaghetti

Dessert $5
Cheesecake, Boston cream pie, sweet kugel, Mimi's Favorite Chocolate Cake,
tapioca or chocolate pudding

Jay Louis, Chef-Owner-King

◖▭◗ *Lady of the House*

Returning to the dining room, I see a group of waiters dressed in black pants, white shirts, and black vests. The waiters are doing their opening side work, which consists of setting tables, organizing the bread station, stacking glassware, and cleaning menus.

"And you are?" A tall, portly, middle-aged man with ginger hair stands in front of me with his eyebrows raised and his hands on his hips.

"I am Mimi Louis." From his outfit, I see that he is a waiter.

"Mimi, darling," the man says. "I've heard so much about you. At last we meet." He clutches his chest. "I am Christopher von Hecht. Everyone calls me Chrissie, although I ask them not to. It is a pleasure to meet you."

So this is the lady of the house.

"I am the senior waiter on the floor," Christopher says. "With the exception of Bette, who is not on the floor but on the counter. And she's off today, which means I'm in charge. Are you here to eat dinner?"

"No," I say, startled by his lack of transition. "I'm here to work, actually."

"Well, there's plenty to do," Christopher says. "We have a party of ten and a party of eight coming in at the same time. School concert, apparently. They will be here at five o'clock and need to be out the door at six-thirty. I don't know who took that reservation, but we don't turn away business, do we? Do you cook?"

"Do I cook?"

"Yes, dear. Do you cook? In other words, will you be in the kitchen doing back of the house work, or will you be with us waiters in the front of the house?"

"Well, I . . ."

"Just trying to allocate resources, squash blossom. Now which is it? Front or back?"

I clear my throat and stand straighter. Chrissie here is doing what all waiters do when confronted with new management. He's making a power play. While I respect his seniority and loyalty to Café Louis, I need to make it clear that Christopher von Hecht works for me. Not the other way around.

"I plan to observe both the back of the house and the front of the house," I say. "It's clear to me that some changes need to made in the restaurant, but I will observe first, before I make any decisions. And I would very much appreciate your input."

Christopher looks down at me and raises an eyebrow. "Of course."

⌗ Restaurant Music

All of a sudden, it's five o'clock and the front door is clogged with people. The two big, back-to-back parties have arrived. Christopher and I get to the door at the same time.

"Good evening," he says. "Welcome to Café Louis. I am Christopher, and this is Mimi. If the Duvall party will follow me, the Gormezano party can follow Mimi."

Christopher has graciously given me the smaller of the two parties, but I am determined to prove my front of the house skills. Pulling menus from the pile, I seat the Gormezano party, take their drink orders, and hand them over to a waiter. Ta da.

After seating half the restaurant, I decide to check on the kitchen. When I open the kitchen door, a cacophony of noise greets me. Pans bang, voices shout, and a tangle of white ordering forms hang from the rack above the heat lamps. I should have realized that the cooks would be overwhelmed. A waitress is yelling for her food. *"¡Oyé, oyé!"* I shout. *"Me llamo Mimi Louis. Soy la hermana de Jeremy. La hija de Jay. ¿Comprenden?"*

Four heads nod at me. I grab the orders and shift them into a pile, guessing when they were delivered by my memory of when I sat the tables. *"Mesa tres,"* I shout. The cooks man their stations and wait for me to call out the dishes. *"No platos primeros. Un sirloin medio rojo. Un pollo Parmesan. Un pollo Marsala."* Looking up, I see the cooks are keeping up with me. *"Mesa catorce. Ensalada Greco . . ."*

Two hours later, I'm still expediting in the kitchen. Sleeves rolled to my biceps, hair tied in a rubber band, and a white apron around my waist, I stand sweating in the kitchen. Working with the four cooks, who introduced themselves as the San Padre brothers, I have almost cleared the board. *"Oyé, por favor. Mesa nueve. Un fettuccine Alfredo. Un flounder. Al lado: tres frites, dos arroz."*

A waitress bangs through the kitchen doors. "I need a

side of mash and a side of rice pilaf on the fly." She turns to leave, her black and red ponytail bouncing.

"Wait for it," I tell her. *"Oyé, por favor. Rápido. Un mash y un arroz."*

"What?" she says to me.

"Wait for it. You put in a fly order, you wait for it."

"I'm totally weeded," she says with her hands on her hips.

"You're weeded?" She has only four tables.

Fly Girl rolls her eyes at me. "Weeded is restaurant talk for being, like, overwhelmed."

"I know." I smile indulgently at her. "I speak restaurant."

Ten minutes after Fly Girl leaves the kitchen, the San Padre brothers put their hands on their hips and wait for more action. *"¡Bueno, bueno!"* I tell them. They smile, proud of their teamwork. Taking off my apron, I head for the dining room.

Because the orders came in all at once and the food went out at a fast clip, everyone is eating at the same time. Scanning the restaurant, I see general calm. Fly Girl looks frantic, swinging her ponytail to and fro, but after watching her for a few moments, I see that hers is self-induced mania. Some servers work better when they are on the edge. It's a buzz, a rush.

Because I am completely disheveled, I don't walk through the dining room. Instead, I stand at one end of the counter and lean against the wall. I'm starting to come down from my kitchen high. Closing my eyes, I listen.

Humming conversation, interspersed with laughter. Knives and forks clicking and clattering. The soft whoosh of the kitchen door opening and closing. Plates chiming as they are cleared from tables. Glasses ringing. This is restaurant music.

■━◀ *Jeremy Louis*

After my day at the restaurant I decided to see my brother. To do so, I had to make an appointment. I look around the anonymous corner office Jeremy maintains as a junior partner in his Philadelphia accounting firm.

My big brother is a very busy man. Always has been. In high school and college, he was president of this, that, and the other thing. Sports, too. Jeremy was captain of West-field High's basketball team. Which was a handy way for me to get boyfriends.

Jeremy gives me the finger. "One minute," he mouths, as he holds up his index finger. I smile and sit myself in one of the chairs facing Jeremy's desk. While Jeremy talks about something financial and boring, I look at him and marvel at our physical differences. Whereas I have Dad's dark hair, skin, and eyes, Jeremy has Mom's light brown hair, green eyes, high cheekbones, and wiry build.

Madeline says that Jeremy is her married crush. "It's not just that Jeremy is good-looking," Madeline told me during a Louis family seder. "Part of his appeal is that he loves his wife and kids. See the way he looks at Allison? That's hot."

I don't know about the hot. One thing is for sure. Jeremy's got it all. Career. Attractive wife. Great kids. Two SUVs. Beautiful house.

At least one of us Louis kids got it right.

Jeremy puts down the phone. "Sorry, Mimi."

Jeremy comes out from behind his desk and gives me a big hug. I always forget how tall he is. Same height as Dad.

"Ally told me about your breakup," Jeremy says. "Are you okay?"

"I will be," I say, pretty sure that I'm not lying.

"What are you going to do with yourself?" Jeremy retreats to his desk and I take a seat in front of it.

"I'm going to run Dad's restaurant," I say.

"What?"

"I'm going to manage Café Louis. It's what I want to do. I think."

"Think harder, Mimi. Running Café Louis isn't a reasonable option."

"Why not?" I ask.

"Because we're selling the restaurant," Jeremy says.

"What?"

"We're selling the restaurant," Jeremy repeats. "We have received a good offer from SHRED to buy the building. SHRED is Schein Real Estate Development. The company is in the process of buying the buildings surrounding Café Louis. SHRED wants to tear down the buildings and build a shopping center."

"Just what the world needs."

Jeremy sifts through piles on his desk until he comes to a manila envelope marked with a purple and red logo. He hands the envelope to me. "We got the offer two weeks ago. My lawyer looked it over and gave it his seal of approval. We just need to sign the papers and it will be a done deal."

"You keep saying 'we,' Jeremy. I had no idea this was happening."

"You haven't been around, Mimi. I didn't think you would care."

"Not care that you are tearing down Dad's restaurant?"

My brother sighs and folds his hands on top of his desk. "Don't get emotional about this. Dad would want us to do what's best for ourselves and our families."

"Right," I say. "And who gets to decide what's best for me? You?"

"You don't seem to be doing a good job of it."

"Hey!"

"I'm sorry," Jeremy says quickly. "I didn't mean that. You're going through a hard time. I'm not trying to make things worse. Listen, Mimi. Selling the restaurant will give us a nice lump sum of cash. You can invest it. I can help."

"Turning a profit at the restaurant would also give us money," I say.

Jeremy exhales. "True. But that would require a lot of time and energy."

"Doesn't she deserve our time and energy? Café Louis is part of our family. How can we just give up on her?"

"Mimi, the restaurant is not a person. It's a property."

"Fine," I say. "That property is half mine."

46

Jeremy frowns. "Ally thinks that selling the restaurant is a good idea."

"Yeah? Well, Ally also thinks it's a good idea for Mom to start dating."

"What?" Jeremy's eyebrows stretch toward his hairline.

"Yep."

Jeremy grimaces. The prospect of Mom dating obviously distresses him. He is silent for a few moments. Then, he shrugs. "Ally usually knows what's best."

"Gag me with a spatula," I say.

Jeremy glares at me, but doesn't respond. Jeremy isn't a fighter. Never has been. Jeremy is the Brandon to my Brenda. "I'm sorry you feel that way" was his answer to any adolescent argument I tried to provoke. Antagonizing Jeremy isn't going to help me now, so I stifle myself.

"Don't you want to relax?" Jeremy says. "Take a vacation? Or at least regroup? You should spend time with Mom."

"I am spending time with Mom. I'm living with her. Remember?"

"I'm serious, Mimi. Mom isn't going to be around for long."

"What do you mean? Is Mom sick?"

"She has high blood pressure," Jeremy says.

"Since when?"

"Mom's getting older. All kinds of things are going to go wrong with her."

I squint at my brother. What's this all about?

Squirming under my squint, Jeremy runs his hands through his hair and changes the subject to our other parent. "Do you want to save Café Louis because you think that's what Dad would want? Because I don't think that's true."

"I'm not doing this for Dad," I say. "I'm doing this for myself. I don't want to take a vacation. I need to find a new life, because my old life just got turned upside down. Café Louis is an oasis of stability."

"Not financial stability," Jeremy says.

"I know Café Louis, and I know restaurants. Why shouldn't I try to rescue her?"

Jeremy starts to chew on his bottom lip. That's Jeremy's tell. When he's questioning himself, he bites his bottom lip. When he's really unsure of himself, he bites both lips.

"What about the people who work at Café Louis?" I continue. "A lot of them have worked for our family for years. Don't we owe them one last try?"

Jeremy keeps chewing his lip, so I keep talking.

"Labor and food costs can be brought down considerably," I add quickly. "I can easily rework the menu to increase check averages."

"You're going to do all of this by yourself?" Jeremy says.

"Madeline will help me," I say. Madeline knows nothing about managing a restaurant. But it sounds better than saying that I will do this work by myself.

"Madeline?" Jeremy says, "The one with all the boyfriends? Isn't she crazy?"

"Not in a bad way."

Jeremy switches his bottom lip for his top lip. I talk faster. "If we do make Café Louis a success, SHRED can build the shopping center around the restaurant. A shopping center would be good, even great. It would increase foot traffic. More customers for us."

Jeremy bites both his lips. I win.

"The Scheins aren't going to be happy about this."

"Tough nougies," I say. "Café Louis is more important than a shopping center."

Jeremy smiles. "We'd have to give it a time limit. Like, three months. If we don't turn a profit by the end of the summer, we sell to the Scheins."

"Summer is the worst season for the restaurant business," I say.

Jeremy raises his eyebrows. "Not up to the challenge?"

"You bet your babka I am. Three months it is." I offer Jeremy my hand. "Deal?"

Jeremy shakes my hand. "Deal."

▬▭◿ *Zucchini*

I'm in Philadelphia, so I might as well get my boxes from Nick's.

Standing on the steps of Nick's row house, I ring the bell and pray that no one answers. Nick should be at the restaurant, which makes this a good time for me to get in, get my stuff, and get gone.

Using my key, I unlock the door and walk into what would've been my home. "Hello?" I call, but the house is empty.

Thankfully, not much of my stuff is here. It's in storage.

We were going to rearrange the closets, then bring over the rest of my clothes. What is here fits into my car. Within fifteen minutes, Sally is packed. Grabbing my mustard collection, I walk out of the house. And right into Nick.

We look at each other, then stare at the ground. "I came to get my stuff," I say.

Nick puts his hands in the pockets of his chef pants. "How are you?"

"Perfect."

"Where are you staying?" Nick asks.

"The Four Seasons."

I sneak a look at Nick's face and see that he is grinning. "I miss having you around," he says. "I miss talking to you about the restaurant. You gave me good advice."

"Oh?" I say. "So now my job is a good thing? You want me for my brains and not my body?"

"You can still come to work at Il Ristorante," Nick says. "With all the publicity hitting, I haven't been around much. Like, now. I had to come home to shower before I go to a cooking class. Since you are in between jobs, I could pay you . . ."

"First of all, I have my own restaurant to worry about," I say.

"Oh, your dad's place?"

"Secondly, you better be careful that promoting the restaurant doesn't get in the way of running the restaurant. Your ass belongs in the kitchen."

"I won't," Nick says. He smiles. "See? You give me good advice."

"Yeah? Well here's another piece of advice," I say.

"Don't dip your zucchini in the house dressing. Ever heard of sexual harassment?"

"Everyone in restaurants fools around with each other. You know that."

"Ironically, I told Claire, my replacement at DI, that she should know everything that goes on in the restaurants she represents. Like that chef in France. He's screwing around on his wife. I know that. But I didn't ever suspect that you were cheating on me. It didn't even occur to me."

"I didn't want it to happen the way it did," Nick says.

"Have you ever read Proverbs, five?"

Nick looks down at his kitchen clogs. "I was going to tell you, in a calm, rational way, that the relationship wasn't working for me. I hoped that you would understand, and agree to work at Il Ristorante."

"That would've worked out well for you. Nice and neat."

"I would like us to be friends," Nick says.

"Maybe we should've been friends before we were lovers. My mom has this theory about taking relationships slowly. But anyway, no. I don't think we can be friends."

"Let me know if you change your mind," Nick says.

"I am changing my mind," I tell him. "I'm changing a lot of things."

❤❤❤ *Allison's Kitchen*

When I tell Mom and Allison that I have Big News, they immediately arrange for a family dinner. As I drive to Allison's house, I think of how pleased Mom will be with my plan to restore Café Louis to her former glory. Surely Mom wants Dad's legacy maintained. I'm less sure about Allison's reaction. She has no sentimental attachment to Café Louis.

No one answers my knock, so I let myself in. I adore this house. If—nay, when—I have a big house, I want it to be like this one. The walls of the foyer are painted pomegranate red. The ceiling is eggshell white, meeting the walls in cream-colored crown molding. The floor is patterned in black and ivory diamonds, and an ornate chandelier descends from the ceiling.

"Hello?" I call, making my way into Allison's kitchen. The kitchen floor is a medley of berry-toned tiles. Above the granite-topped island hangs a canopy of pots and pans. The stainless steel Sub-Zero refrigerator stands in front of a Viking stove and six-burner range. Light wood cabinets are fronted by glass, bringing light into the kitchen and revealing Allison's neatly arranged plates, bowls, glasses, and mugs. French doors lead to the backyard, where I see a giant play center for the kids.

"Aunt Mimi!" Gideon and Ezra jump around my knees and I lean down to receive their apple-juiced kisses. They are still young enough to be unselfconsciously affectionate.

My niece, Sarah, is different. A very mature eight-year-old, she is the young lady her mother raises her to be. Sarah kisses my cheek, then puts her hand in mine. Sarah has her mother's blond hair, but there is something of my father in her face. Something wise. "Mom said that a boy made you very sad. But I'm glad you're home."

"Thank you, sweetie." I adore this child. I should spend more time with her.

With a mouthful of lasagna, Jeremy says, "Mimi doesn't want to sell Café Louis. She wants to run it for three months to see if she can make it profitable. If not, we sell to SHRED."

I'm wondering where the "we" went—as in "we agreed not to sell the restaurant"—when Mom says, "I think that's a big mistake."

I crunch my brow in Mom's direction. She says, "I thought your big news was that you found a job."

"I did find a job," I say. "Not a new job. An old job."

Mom says, "If you want to run your own restaurant, you should sell Café Louis and use the money to buy your own place."

"We have a restaurant up and running. She just needs a few changes to be profitable. Why would I start from scratch?"

Mom exhales loudly. "What do you think, Ally?"

Allison wipes a blob of tomato sauce from Gideon's face. "I don't know anything about the restaurant business."

"But you must have an opinion," Mom pushes.

Why does she care so much about what Allison thinks?

Allison shrugs. "If Mimi really wants this . . ."

"I do."

". . . then I guess we should support her."

"Great. Thanks." I'll take it.

◼▭◖ *M&M's*

Seeking more validation, I invite Madeline to The Garden. "Take the Ben Franklin Bridge to Route 108. Make a left at the Home Depot. Turn right at the Dunkin' Donuts. Bear right at the Starbucks. You'll pass Target, McDonald's and Burger King. Turn left at the Dunkin' Donuts, right at the Starbucks and after the Home Depot, turn left on Kean Road and you'll see the sign for The Garden. The address is 32 Tomato Road."

Madeline arrives wearing three-inch mules, camo pants, and a white tank top. I can see both her bra and her biceps. Madeline hands me a white box. "Your favorite," she says.

Inside the pink and white Tiers box is a piece of vanilla sponge cake filled with kirsch mousseline. *"Merci mucho,"* I say.

She smiles. "Who's your Maddie?"

We sit on Mom's cream-colored couch. Maddie picks up *SJ* magazine and starts to leaf through it. I clear my throat and say, "Maddie, I'm going to run my dad's restaurant."

Madeline puts down the magazine.

While I tell Madeline about my plans to revitalize Café Louis, she picks at a scar on her forearm. Madeline has scars up and down her arms. They are a result of her years working in professional kitchens. Hot liquids, knives, and ovens have left their mark on her. Of course, Madeline has other scars that aren't visible.

"What do you think of my plan?" I ask.

Madeline shrugs. "You're the restaurant consultant. I'm just a cook."

"You're not just a cook," I say.

Madeline shrugs. "It seems to me like backward momentum. Still, I am your friend and I'll support you."

"Thanks. I'm overwhelmed."

To catch some spring sunshine, we move into Mom's courtyard garden. I sit in one of the outdoor club chairs. Madeline pulls a pair of purple sunglasses from her bag. Like a cat in the sun, Madeline stretches her limbs on a chaise longue. She smiles at me. "Where are we with the Nick fallout?"

"I'm still in the sulk," I say. "Let's face it. I'm homeless, jobless, and manless. I can figure out the living situation and the employment issue, but I hate being single. It sucks."

"I don't think singledom sucks," Madeline says. "I like my freedom."

"I don't want freedom. I want a mortgage and a diaper bag."

Madeline sifts through her hot pink tote. "I thought I put sunscreen in here."

"What I'm thinking is that I need to change myself in order to get what I want. Maybe I need to be more feminine."

Madeline says, "What is feminine?"

"I don't know. Less tigery, more kittenish."

Madeline kicks off her mules. "Don't get all damsel-in-distress, Mimi. It doesn't become you."

"I don't know how to damsel. But there's an in between,

isn't there? Look at Ally. Hair, makeup, attitude. Ally is so well done. I'm too raw."

"Not raw." Madeline waves her hands in the air. "Rare. As in special. You're a filet mignon, cooked rare."

"Filet mignon? I feel like a day-old Big Mac."

"You'll find a man who can savor your rareness. Speaking of which, you should get back in someone's saddle. Don't let living with Bobbi turn you into a nun."

"I am not in the mood for sex. My diva has laryngitis."

"My diva is singing arias," Madeline says. "The lawyer I'm sleeping with is quite the conductor."

"Good for you."

Madeline smiles. "Yes. It is good for me."

Lipstick Theory Two

We are heckling chefs on the Food Network when Mom comes home. "Hi, girls," she greets us.

Madeline rises from the couch to hug Mom. "You look very nice, Bobbi," Madeline says. Mom is wearing a pale peach, lightweight sweater and a cream-colored skirt that shows off her legs. And yes, Madeline calls my mother by her first name. Mom prefers it.

"Thank you, Maddie." Mom walks to her computer. "My friends and I went to a matinee performance of a new play at Arden Theater. We're going to get a bite to eat. I'm just going to check the e-mail and I'll be out of your way. I need to see if any men have contacted me."

"Men?" Madeline asks.

"I joined an Internet dating site for people over fifty."

"Good for you, Bobbi." Madeline pokes my arm. "You're lucky to have such a cool mom."

"I am cool, aren't I?" Then Mom sighs. "No e-mails."

"Don't be discouraged," Madeline says. "These things take time. Dating is rough."

"Mom, tell Maddie your lipstick theory."

Mom turns off her computer and turns to us. "My lipstick theory is that you should always wear lipstick because you never know who you're going to meet."

"Mom! That is not your lipstick theory."

"It's not?" Mom says. "What is it? I forget."

"You compared dating to shopping for lipstick. You said that we should go slowly and date carefully, just like we try on a lot of lipsticks before we buy one."

Madeline grins. "I buy all the lipsticks."

⌦ The Make-Up Bar

"Look at them," Allison says as she waves her hand in front of my eyes. She's gesturing to my overgrown eyebrows, showing them to Lisa Severino, waxer extraordinaire. Allison insisted on bringing me to The Make-Up Bar so she could properly introduce me to Lisa, whom she described as her WMD in the war on hair.

Lisa looks at my face, and I look at hers. She is perfectly cosmeticked and coiffed. Lisa is an Italian-American version of my perfect sister-in-law. I feel vastly inadequate. But Lisa smiles. "It's not that bad," she says.

While Lisa applies the wax, Allison busies herself among the makeup samples. The salon is busy with hairstylists and manicurists, and a bevy of women wait for Lisa to wax them. Meanwhile, I blink back tears as Lisa whisks the wax from my face.

"Look." Lisa offers me a hand mirror. In the harsh but natural light pouring in through The Make-Up Bar's windows, I see only the wrinkles around my eyes. Then I raise the mirror and see two well-arched brows. My eyes look bigger and my nose looks smaller. What a difference a wax makes.

"It's all about balance," Lisa says.

∈══⊃ *Bette's Counter*

"I heard it, but I didn't believe it," says Bette when I walk into Café Louis that afternoon.

"For better or for worse." I approach the counter. "I'm here."

"For the better, hon. Come here and give me a hug."

Bette is one of Café Louis's original waitresses. Now Bette is near sixty. She's still rail thin. What dates Bette is her Reagan-era makeup. Bette's eyelids are weighted with blue shadow and her lashes struggle against black mascara. She wears pink, frosted lipstick. "Bette," I say. "I've missed you terribly."

I have. When I was a child, Bette was the most glamorous woman in my world. She'd breeze into the restaurant on a cloud of Jean Naté and cigarette smoke, her lipstick smeared from kissing goodbye her latest boyfriend, whose Firebird or TransAm squealed and roared as it left the parking lot.

"I work the counter now," she tells me with pride. "Since your dad got sick, I've been keeping my eye on things." Bette smiles. "But now you're here. Things are going to get better. I just know it."

Bette's counter is filled with regulars by five o'clock. I watch Bette with admiration as she kibitzes with her mostly male audience. "It's Friday, Hugh. You think I don't know that you want the meatloaf?"

That night, after the other servers have left, Bette and I sit at the counter drinking coffee, sharing a piece of chocolate cake and talking. I tell her my plans for Café Louis. "That all sounds great," Bette says. "Now tell me about the jerk boyfriend."

I give her the Nick synopsis. She says, "Men never know what they want, do they?"

◧━━⬱ Menu Madness

Madeline is late to the meeting I have called to discuss the changes I want to make to Café Louis. I can't be mad at Madeline because she is coming straight from Tiers, and because she has volunteered to come for moral support.

Grammy Jeff slowly walks to the tables I have pushed together for our meeting. She is tired. I can see it in her eyes, and her shoulders. "How y'all doin'?" Grammy says when she sits in the chair next to her grandson.

"How are you feeling, Grammy?" Bette asks. I realize that Bette and Grammy are within five years of each other. As is my mom.

"I'm doing just fine," Grammy answers. She reaches for the white container that holds packets of sweetener. Grammy pulls five white packets of sugar.

Nelson grabs the sugar out of Grammy's hand. He replaces the white packets with pink packets. Grammy frowns at her grandson. "Nellie, I want some sugar in my tea."

"You had sugar in your tea an hour ago," Nelson says. "I saw you."

"Nellie . . ."

Nelson interrupts her. "Don't make me come at you with the insulin."

"Here I am," Madeline says as she bounds through the door.

Introducing Madeline, I go around the table and realize that the staff has divided themselves into two teams. Representing the kitchen are Grammy Jeff and Nelson. The front of the house representatives are Christopher and Bette.

"Pleased to meet you all," Madeline says cheerfully. She puts two bakery boxes on the table.

"What's that?" Nelson asks, peering inside the first box.

"Cream puffs," Madeline answers. "We were making a croquembouche. It's a traditional French wedding cake made out of cream puffs. You stack them to make a four-foot tower, then caramelize sugar over the whole thing to enclose it. The bride and groom take a champagne bottle and swing at the tower, cracking the sugar. It's pretty cool. Anyway, I brought these because we made too many cream puffs."

"No such thing as too many cream puffs," Christopher says.

Madeline smiles at him, then opens the second box. "These are chocolate samples from different suppliers. Tell me what you think."

"What happened to Franco at Le Chocolat?" I ask.

"He cheated on me," Madeline says. "He said that he was importing his unsweetened chocolate just for me. Yesterday I found out that he's been selling to Aux Petit Delices behind my back. I had to break up with him. I mean, I have my pride."

"I like my chocolate like I like my men," Christopher says.

"Dark?" Nelson asks.

"French," Christopher replies. "And not too bitter."

"Can we start the meeting please?" I say.

Christopher nods at me. "Start your meeting, pea pod."

"As you may have heard, Café Louis has not been profitable for some time. A real estate developer has made an offer to buy the property. But I think we can turn around the restaurant and restore her to her former glory. I have some ideas on how to do that, but I'd like your input."

Grammy Jeff says, "If it's a good offer, maybe you should sell the restaurant."

"Not without a fight," I state.

"Who are you fighting?" Grammy asks.

Bette says, "Tell us your ideas, Mimi."

"Increase check averages by reformatting the menu. Right now, there's no section for appetizers. We need fried calamari. Nachos. As we add dishes, I want to remove the ones that don't sell. From what I've seen of the past three months' ordering slips, we should remove the chicken cordon bleu, meatloaf, and broiled flounder."

"Hugh will have a fit." Bette shakes her head. "He orders meatloaf every Friday."

"Hugh ordering the meatloaf once a week doesn't justify having it on the menu," I explain. "Also, I want to go to an à la carte menu. Right now, each entree comes with soup or salad and two sides. We're giving away food."

"Oy." Christopher rolls his eyes.

"Our customers won't like that," Bette says.

"We will fill each plate with a starch and veg," I continue. "Everything will be portion-controlled to lower costs. Which is the next thing. I'm going to find new suppliers so we can lower our food costs."

"This sounds fabulous," Christopher drawls, "but the waiters are the ones who will have to explain these changes to the customers."

"I'll back you up," I say.

"Who's going to back you up?" Christopher asks.

"Mimi can hold her own in any restaurant," Madeline says.

"Your father would be proud of you," Bette says. "Welcome home."

Café Louis

Family owned and operated since 1970

Starters

Chicken Fingers $5   Fried Calamari $6   Mozzarella Sticks $6
Nachos San Padre $8 *with meat or chicken, salsa fresca, cheese, sour cream,
and homemade guacamole*

Soup and Salad

Soup of the Season $6   French Onion Soup $5   Jersey Clam Chowder $5

Mimi's Seasonal Salad $6   Greek Salad $5   Caesar Salad $5
Add grilled chicken $7   Add shrimp $9

Entrees

Linguini & Meatballs $10
Fettuccine Alfredo $10
Lasagne $10
Grilled Chicken in Summer Vegetable Ragout $12
Arroz con Pollo $12
N.Y. Strip Steak $15
Jay's Brisket $12
Mussels & Linguine $12
Shrimp Scampi $12
Grilled Jersey Tuna in White Wine–Mustard Sauce $15

Sides $3

Vegetable of the day   Mash of the day   French Fries
Baked Potato   Seasonal Vegetable Slaw Rice Pilaf

Children $5

Chicken Fingers & French Fries   Grilled Cheese   Linguine & Meatballs

Dessert $5

Louis Family Cheesecake   Crème Brûlée   Chocaholic Triple Layer Cake
Basset's Ice Cream of the Week   Jersey Peach Pie   Jersey Berry Cobbler

All menu items are available to take out.
Ask for our catering menu!

▭━◁ *Family Business, Part One*

"Is Jeremy here?" A man my age smiles across the counter at me. He looks like a typical suburban guy. Average height. Barbered, blond hair. Brown eyes. Khakis and a pale pink button-down shirt. The requisite cell phone is clipped to his belt. He's holding a giant Styrofoam cup of Dunkin' Donuts coffee. He's nice-looking, but so generic that he might as well have an SKU on his forehead.

"Jeremy's not here. Can I help you with something? I'm his sister."

"Ah. There's absolutely no family resemblance. Which I mean as a compliment. I'm Aaron."

Smiling, I say, "I'm Mimi. You're a friend of Jeremy's?"

"Acquaintance. Since I'm here . . ." He gestures to the counter.

"Please," I say. "Have a seat."

Aaron sits at the counter and points to Hugh. "What's up with him?"

"He's protesting." Hugh is eating and enjoying grilled chicken with summer vegetable ragout. However, he holds a sign in front of his plate. "Bring back the meatloaf."

I hand a menu to Aaron. He nods as he reads the new menu. "I'm impressed. You made everything sound delicious."

"I was a restaurant consultant for many years. Time to bring it all home."

"The joy and pain of a family-run business," Aaron says. "Just when you think you're out, they pull you back in."

I laugh. "I guess it depends on the family business."

"As it turns out, Mimi, we have something in common. I also work for my family's business."

"What's your family's business?" I ask.

Aaron says, "You are very pretty."

That catches me off-guard. "Thank you. Stress must look good on me."

"Tell me your troubles and I'll make them go away."

"I doubt that."

"Tell me one trouble," Aaron says. "And I hope it doesn't involve a boyfriend."

"No boyfriend trouble. No boyfriend."

"Good. Then what is your stress?"

I shrug. "Business."

"Well," Aaron says. "Your business can be my business."

I smile. "My business is none of your business."

"Actually," Aaron says, "it is."

"Oh?"

"One thing you'll love about me," Aaron says, "is that I don't lie."

"Is that right?"

"It is. I spoke the truth. Your business can be my business. If you sell it to me."

Then, I understand. "You're a Schein."

"The son Schein. Aaron Schein. Pleased to meet you."

Bette approaches, ordering pad at the ready.

"Enjoy your meal." I walk into the kitchen.

* * *

Much to my discontent, Aaron seems unperturbed by my exit. In fact, he seems quite at home in the restaurant, greeting the servers, talking to other counter customers. He eats with gusto, telling his counter neighbors that the food is fabulous. Everyone seems to like Aaron. This irritates me.

When he has cleaned his plate and wiped his mouth, Aaron waits at the register to pay his bill. Which means that I have to accept his money. Dookie.

"Everything to your liking?" I ask breezily as I punch the register.

"There was one thing missing," Aaron says.

"What?" I ask, alarmed.

"Your company," he answers with what really is a very nice smile. I return the smile and hand Aaron his change. Looking him in the eye, I say, "You're not going to get your hands on my company."

Undeterred, Aaron says, "It was a pleasure meeting you, Mimi Louis."

◼━◁ Egg Creams & Drive-In Movies

The smell of Mom's perfume draws me into her bedroom. Mom stands in front of her television. She points. "Look who it is."

I look and see Nick. Dressed in immaculate chef whites, Nick is cooking with the host of a local TV show. "Putz," Mom says and snaps off the television.

Smiling at Mom, I see that she's dressed in a champagne-colored sheath dress. "Going out?" I ask as I belly-flop onto her bed.

"Yes," Mom says. "I have a date."

"What?" I sit up. "With who?"

"Sid."

"Who's Sid?"

"From the website," Mom says. "We spoke on the phone a few nights ago and had a very pleasant conversation. We're meeting tonight for dinner."

"You're jumping straight to dinner? Shouldn't you meet for a drink first?"

Mom takes off one necklace and puts on another. "I'm not a big drinker."

"The point is not to drink. The point is not to get stuck with someone for a long time. Listen, Mom. I've dated a lot more than you have. Let me explain how it works. First, you meet for a drink or coffee. For, like, half an hour. To see if you like each other."

Mom says, "How am I supposed to decide if I like someone in half an hour?"

"Don't you just know?"

"I don't know," Mom says.

"Did you arrange for a safety call?"

"A what?"

"Safety call. You have someone call you half an hour into the date. If you want to leave, you feign an emergency. If not, you stay."

Mom puts on an open-toed slingback and looks in the mirror. "I think I can spare two hours out of my life."

"I'm trying to prepare you for the modern dating world," I say. "It can be rough. At any age. It's not egg creams and drive-in movies anymore."

Mom smiles. "Maybe it should be."

⬛━◗ Hunter Farm

Sally is not happy with me. She's getting very dirty. Mud spatters her sides and cakes onto her wheels as we bump along a back road. "We're almost there," I tell Sally.

Where we almost are is Hunter Farm, from which I intend to buy juicy Jersey produce. Sitting at a red light on Church Road in Westfield, I think about the childhood I spent here. Farms. Woods. Now Westfield is developed. Overdeveloped, like a thirteen-year-old girl wearing a DD bra.

There's no sign indicating the farm, but the dirt road leads me and Sally to a stone and brick house with a wide porch. It looks freshly painted and there are cute gingham curtains in the windows. Cats roam around the porch, and a dog barks when I get out of my car. Inhaling, I smell the air. It smells green.

"Hello?" I call through the screen door of the house.

A tiny woman comes out of the house's shadows. Her white hair is pinned into a neat bun and her brown eyes glow with kindness. "Hello, dear," she says.

"Are you Mrs. Hunter?" I ask politely.

"Yes," she says, and smooths her flowered housedress. She clearly is not expecting company.

"I'm Mimi Louis. I called yesterday? Joe said I should come by and see the farm. I'm looking for produce for my restaurant."

"Come in, dear," she says, pushing open the screen door.

Following Mrs. Hunter through the front room of the house, I see that it is neat, but shabby. The wood floors look clean, but the area rugs are worn. The furniture is solid and antiquish. A chocolate leather chair is in the corner next to a burgundy wing chair. The room is dark, with drops of sunlight peeking through the white curtains.

"Joe's out in the field," Mrs. Hunter says as she leads me into the kitchen. It's a big kitchen with an ash wood table and chairs, white cabinets fronted with frosted glass, a large white refrigerator, and a separate freezer. Knickknacks stand on shelves and flowered curtains hang from brass rods on the windows. The kitchen is filled with sunshine.

"Have a seat," Mrs. Hunter says, and I sit at the kitchen table. Mrs. Hunter moves to the kitchen cabinets. She places a delicate china cup, saucer, and spoon in front of me. From the refrigerator, Mrs. Hunter retrieves a porcelain cow filled with milk. She gets a glass bowl of sugar from the cabinet, and sets these things before me. "Here you are, dear."

"Thank you." There is no coffee in my cup, or anywhere in sight. I decide not to mention this.

Mrs. Hunter sits across from me. "Are you a friend of Joe's?"

Didn't I already explain what I'm doing here? Maybe I

didn't. "I'm here to see the farm. I'm looking for produce for my restaurant."

Mrs. Hunter nods. "Joe's been working hard since he came back to the farm."

"Came back from where?"

"France. Italy." Mrs. Hunter smiles, seemingly proud of her son's travels.

Nodding politely, I say, "Will Joe be back soon or should I go look for him?"

"Would you like a muffin?" Mrs. Hunter asks brightly, getting to her feet before I answer. "Joe says I have to stop baking so much now that it's just the two of us here. My husband passed on." Mrs. Hunter places a plate of muffins before me. I see that she is wearing her wedding ring.

"I'm sorry," I say.

"Me, too." Mrs. Hunter touches her hand to the silver cross around her neck. From beneath her housedress, Mrs. Hunter pulls another silver chain, around which is a man's gold wedding band. She kisses the ring. "I miss him every day."

Mrs. Hunter's sentimentality touches my heart. Smiling, I bite into a blueberry muffin. "Delicious," I tell Mrs. Hunter with my mouth full. She beams in delight.

"Tell me, dear," Mrs. Hunter says, "Are you a friend of Joe's?"

■━━⊏ *Farmer Joe*

Fifteen long minutes later, the back door creaks open, then bangs shut. I hear the thud of boots on wood. A man's voice calls, "Mom?"

I smell him before I see him. Into the clean, bright kitchen wafts the aroma of male sweat mingled with the pungent smell of sod.

"In the kitchen, dear," Mrs. Hunter calls. To me, she says, "Here comes my Joe." She rises slowly to her feet and smooths her dress, smiling in anticipation of seeing her son. Or does she think it's her husband?

Into the kitchen comes Joe Hunter. He's wearing work boots, faded jeans, and a navy short sleeved T-shirt. There's a baseball hat on his head and he's looking down at his mother, so I can't see his face. "Hi, Mom," he says, and kisses her cheek. Then he looks up and sees me. "Hello."

Joe takes off his hat and runs his fingers through his wheat-colored hair, which hangs past his ears. Joe has the same warm, iced tea–colored eyes as his mother. His face is long, like his body, and there's stubble on his jaw.

"Oh," Mrs. Hunter says, as if seeing me for the first time. "We have company." I watch her eyes move to my coffee cup and the muffins. She sees that I have been here with her for some time. Mrs. Hunter chews on her bottom lip. She's trying to remember who I am and what I'm doing in her kitchen. To save time and embarrassment, I stand and tell Joe, "I'm Mimi Louis. I called yesterday?"

"Yes," Mrs. Hunter says. "Mimi. She's a friend of yours," she tells Joe.

Without confirming or correcting his mother, Joe leans down and kisses Mrs. Hunter's forehead.

Joe leads me through the house and out the back door. The planting rows begin a quarter of a mile from the Hunters' back door. The first few rows are strawberry plants. They hunch close to the ground, their growth stunted by the weight of hanging strawberries. Beyond the strawberries lies furrowed ground with greenery popping out of the brown dirt. Following Joe past the strawberry plants, I inhale. The air is sweet. It smells red.

A dog of indeterminate breed bounds out of a shed and heads straight toward me, barking madly. "Good job," Joe says to the dog. "She's only been here for half an hour."

Laughing, I extend my hand for the dog to sniff. The dog smells my hand, licks it, then rolls onto his back and squirms around on the ground, his canine member quite noticeably erect. It flops from side to side as the dog squirms.

Joe shakes his head. "This is not the way to impress a woman. How many times have I told you? You gotta play it cool, son."

"Does he do this with all the girls?"

"No," Joe says. "Just the pretty ones."

Well, now. A flirtatious farmer.

Walking toward the greenhouses, Joe slows his pace to walk beside me and explain the system for the farm. "The greenhouses used to be for baby lettuces," he says. "The farm specialized in that stuff for a few years. Do you know about baby lettuce?"

Do I know about baby lettuce? "Yes."

Joe nods. "My dad built these greenhouses to grow baby lettuces, but it turned out to be too labor-intensive to be profitable. You have to snip the beds of lettuce every other day, put the lettuce in airtight plastic, and get it to the customer within twelve hours before it starts to wilt." Joe shakes his head. "Sissy food."

Stopping at the door to the greenhouse, Joe turns and looks down at me, narrowing his eyes and smiling. "Please don't tell me you came here for baby lettuce."

"No," I laugh. "No sissy food for me."

"Whew." Joe holds open the door of the greenhouse. Into the gaseous hothouse we go. Joe starts explaining the photosynthesis that is taking place in the greenhouse. From working with other farmers, I already know about accelerating the growth of plants. But I don't interrupt Joe. His voice is lyrical and reedy, and he obviously enjoys explaining his work.

"I'm using the greenhouses to grow small batches of produce and experiment with them before I plant big crops of them. See? These are heirloom tomatoes."

"Pretty," I say, knowing full well what heirlooms are. "But if you grow them in greenhouse conditions, how can you be sure that the plants will thrive in the outdoors?"

Joe smiles. "If I treat the earth right, she might tell me her secrets."

Joe shows me the other greenhouses, and the barn. The barn is dark, the warm sun seeping through slats in the wood. Peeking into bins and barrels, I say, "Nice ramps. Those are great-looking morels. Are those the last of the fiddleheads? I might have to steal them. Fiddleheads, ramps, morels, and a nice piece of halibut. Sounds like supper."

Joe smiles. "You have an educated palate."

"I eat a lot."

Joe looks me up and down. "Wouldn't know it."

Walking to the side of the barn, I spot bins of freshly cut herbs. Holding a bunch of herbs to my nose, I say, "Chervil?"

"Good call," Joe says.

"Let's see. I could add garlic to the chervil, hit it with white wine, kiss it with fresh tomato sauce, and drizzle it over my halibut."

"Are you flirting with me?" Joe says.

"What? No."

Joe says, "What time should I come over for dinner?"

"Please. I live with my mother."

Joe smiles. "So do I."

That makes me laugh. Joe takes a step toward me. The smell of his sweat overpowers the smell of the chervil. I take a purposeful step backward, then say, "I am impressed with your produce, Farmer Joe. I like it. I like it a lot."

Joe smiles. "I'm glad you're excited about it."

Sheepishly, I say, "It's been a while since I've had good food to play with."

"Play," Joe says. "I like that. Play."

"Cook, I mean."

"I know what you mean." Joe leans against the wall of the barn and I see the sinewy muscles of his arms.

The diva whispers something that I choose not to hear.

Walking half a mile back to the shed which serves as his office, Joe tells me about ordering and delivery procedures. We walk past a shed filled with barrels. The barrels are marked with the names of some of the best restaurants in Philadelphia. "What's in there?" I ask.

"We have special arrangements with some restaurants," Joe says. "Chefs want items grown specifically for them. A certain color potato, or fruit picked at a certain time. My dad started the service. I'd like to discontinue it, but we make a lot of profit from it." Joe walks past the shed and continues to his office. He hasn't bragged about having chichi restaurants as clients. I like that.

In his office, Joe hands me order forms and a credit application. "If you decide to work with us, fax all this crap back to me," he says. "Or bring it back personally."

Joe walks me around the house, toward Sally. "Is that your car?"

"Yep."

He puts his hands in the pockets of jeans. "Mustang GT with a Shelby scoop, flared deck lid, and front valance. A 1966?"

"Yes, sir. Four-speed Toploader transmission and a 289 HIPO engine."

Joe looks me up and down. "You like Mustangs?"

"I like this one." I get behind the wheel.

"Well," Joe says. "If you drive a car like this, you must be some kinda woman."

"You judge people by the cars they drive?"

"Always." Joe smiles.

"So what do you drive?"

Joe grins. "A tractor."

Driving away from Hunter Farm, I can't get the smell of Joe's sweat out of my nose. His sweat smelled like onions. No. Leeks. No. Scallions.

He's quite manly, the diva says. Earthy. Yummy.

That may be, but do I want to date a farmer? Think of the mud.

Yes, the diva says. Think of the mud.

No, don't think of the mud. Don't think about him at all. Did I learn nothing from Nick? There needs to be more to a relationship than physical attraction.

The diva doesn't answer.

➤ *Pie*

On my way back to Café Louis, I call Madeline. It's three o'clock and she's leaving work. "What do you know about Joe Hunter from Hunter Farm?" I ask.

"He died," Madeline says.

"Not the father," I say. "The son."

"There's a son?"

Big help she is. "What's new with you?"

Madeline says, "I broke up with the lawyer."

"What happened?"

"The other night, he came into the bedroom with a can of Reddi-wip. He wanted to put it on me and lick it off. I said, 'First of all, I'm a chef. I'm covered in food all day. It's not a turn-on for me. Secondly, I'm a pastry chef. No one is putting some cheap-ass, canned whipped cream on me.'"

"And he took offense to that?"

Madeline ignores my sarcasm. "Tonight I'm going out with a guy I met during The Book & The Cook preview party. He's a civilian, not a chef. I should tell him the whipped cream rule before he goes and gets any ideas."

"A whipped cream conversation on a first date?"

Madeline says, "I slept with him after the party, so this is our second date."

"Madeline."

"You know me," she says. "I'm as easy as pie."

100 Simple Rules for Dating My Mother

When I get home from the restaurant that night, Mom's car is in the driveway. "Mom?" I call when I walk in the door. There's no answer. "Mom?" I walk through the condo. Mom isn't home. I take off my dirty restaurant clothes and get in the shower to wash away the smell of grease.

Thirty minutes later, it's 10 P.M. and Mom still isn't home. It's strange that her car is here but she isn't. I call Mom's cell phone. It rings, but she doesn't answer, so I leave a voice mail for her to call me.

At 11 P.M., I get mildly concerned and call Jeremy. My brother does a full-on freak. "What if she went out with some Internet pervert? Who has she been e-mailing?"

"I don't know," I say.

"Why not?"

"Because I don't invade her privacy," I say. "And I'm trying to ignore the fact that she is dating."

"You live with her, Mimi. I thought you were going to be responsible." Jeremy turns his mouth from the phone and I hear him say, "Allison, I told you that it's a bad idea for Mom to date."

"Ease up on the panic, Jeremy. I didn't call to alarm you. I called to see if she was at your house. Don't worry. Mom will turn up eventually."

"Eventually?" Jeremy says. "That's not good enough. I'm coming over, and if we don't hear from Mom by midnight, we'll call the police."

At 11:45 P.M., the front door opens. Jeremy says, "Mom? Is that you? Are you okay?"

"Jeremy?" Mom says. "What are you doing here?" As an answer, Jeremy wraps Mom in a bear hug. Mom looks confused, but returns his hug.

"Mimi?" she says. "What's going on?"

Hands on my hips, I say, "You've got some explaining to do."

Mom sits at the kitchen table, hanging her head. Jeremy and I stand, arms folded across our chests. "You're right," Mom says. "I'm sorry."

Mom was at the Phillies game with Sid. The game went into extra innings. Because of the noise of the stadium, Mom didn't hear her phone ring.

"I was a little worried. Jeremy was doing a full-on hissy dance."

"If you're going to date," Jeremy says, "you need to be more responsible."

"You're right," Mom says for the tenth time.

"We should make some ground rules," I suggest. "So we're all on the same page."

"Good idea," Jeremy says, and proceeds to make the rules. "The first rule is that you tell Ally, me, or Mimi where you are going and with whom."

"Okay," Mom says.

"Also," Jeremy says. "You should take your own car on dates until you've been out with someone a few times."

Mom laughs. "That's a little silly."

"It's not silly, Mom," I say. "Do you know how many stories I've heard about psychos on the Internet?"

Mom waves her hand in the air. "These are old Jewish men."

"How do you know?" Jeremy says. "Anyone can put up a photo and a profile. Who you think is a sixty-five-year-old retired teacher could be a twenty-three-year-old with a roll of duct tape and a fetish for older women."

Mom stops laughing.

"We want you to be safe," Jeremy says.

"You're our one and only mommy," I add, hoping to water down Jeremy's worry.

"You're right." Mom nods. "I'll follow your rules."

"Good," Jeremy says.

"Now go to your room," I say.

The next morning, banging wakes me. When I stagger into the kitchen, Mom says, "Oh, good. You're up." She gestures to bowls and measuring cups on the kitchen counter. "I made pancakes. From scratch."

"Are those guilt pancakes?"

"With sorry syrup," Mom answers. As I make coffee, Mom turns the heat on under a griddle on the stove. As she ladles batter onto the griddle, she says, "I really like Sid."

"Mom, you don't have to tell me this." I hope she won't continue. She does.

"He's very special. Smart. Cultured. Romantic." Mom waves her spatula in the air. "He's not gorgeous but he's not ugly."

I say, "He's no Billy Crystal."

"Sadly, no." Mom smiles. "But we're going out again tonight. And tomorrow night."

"Don't rush into anything."

"Mimi, I'm sixty years old. I don't rush anywhere."

▭▬◁ *Mutiny*

The next night, Aaron Schein comes into Café Louis. From the kitchen, I watch Aaron take a seat at the counter. Bette takes his order. When she walks into the kitchen, I jump her. "What'd he order?"

"The New York strip and a baked potato."

"Give him the grilled tuna," I tell her. "And French fries."

She does, and when Aaron sees his dinner, he smiles. "Did Mimi think I'd like this?" he asks loudly. "How sweet of her. Isn't she sweet?"

Dagnabit.

The next day, Aaron comes in for dinner. He orders lasagna. I have Bette serve him nachos. While Aaron eats, Bette leans over the counter and talks to him. She laughs, smooths her hair, and winks at him before moving to other customers.

"What are you doing?" I ask when she comes into the kitchen.

Bette smiles. "If you're not going to flirt with him, I will."

By the third day, word of Aaron's persistent pursuit has spread through the wait staff. When he arrives for dinner, Aaron is greeted at the front door by Christopher von Hecht. This makes me incredibly nervous, because I'm not sure whose side Christopher is on.

Christopher leads Aaron to a booth, then turns his back to the kitchen door, blocking my view. They speak for quite some time. When Christopher comes into the kitchen, I grab his arm. "Chrissie, what are you doing?"

"Calm down, peanut butter cup. I'm doing my job."

"Right." I release his arm. "You took Aaron's order. Because you're his waiter."

"That's one of my jobs." Christopher hangs the order on the rack in front of the San Padre brothers. Then he turns to me. "My other job is to marry you off to a nice Jewish man."

"That is not your job," I say, hands planted firmly on hips.

"I'm a matchmaker." Christopher shrugs. "It's what I was born to do."

"Since when?"

"Since now. Whose food is this?" Christopher looks at the plates piling up in the window. *"¿Hombres, que mesa?"*

"Nueve," someone answers.

I say, "Aaron is not a good match for me. He's trying to ruin this restaurant."

"That's not true and you know it." Christopher arranges the plates on a large serving tray. "Aaron's family made your family what I assume was a perfectly good offer to buy the property. If it wasn't a good offer, your brother—who is clearly the more levelheaded sibling—wouldn't have considered it. This isn't a family feud. It's a business deal. You're no Juliet and I'm not Richard Dawson."

"What?"

"Think on that." Christopher hoists the tray to his shoulder and leaves.

On the fourth night, Aaron comes into the restaurant with a young, blond woman. They sit at a table in Fly Girl's section. When Fly Girl comes into the kitchen with their order, I ask to see it. Shared mozzarella sticks to start, followed by New York strip steak and a chicken Caesar, which is presumably for the girl. Narrowing my eyes, I say, "This is date food."

"Yup," Fly Girl agrees.

"Fine." I shrug. "I don't care."

"Of course you don't." Fly Girl nods. "But if you do, you should act like you don't."

Do I care? Being pursued was annoying. And nice. Has Aaron given up already?

Smiling, I breeze out of the kitchen and through the dining room. "Good evening," I greet the customers, and offer a polite nod and smile to Aaron. "Good evening, Mr. Schein. Lovely to see you again."

"Miss Louis." Aaron returns my nod as I float past him.

An hour later, Fly Girl pulls me aside. "They are sharing a dessert."

"Whatever." So, Aaron Schein has a thinner-than-me, younger-than-me girlfriend. Good for him.

I'm standing at the door when Aaron and his harlot leave. "I hope everything was to your liking," I say in my best fake voice.

Aaron fakes me right back. "Delicious as always."

The twig squeaks, "It was very good."

Aaron smiles. "Mimi, this is Amanda. My sister."

"Sister?" I blurt.

"Sister," Aaron repeats, a grin growing on his face.

"Oh. Of course. Your sister."

"Jealous?" Aaron's brown eyes twinkle.

"No."

"My heart belongs to you, Mimi Louis. Whether you choose to possess it or not."

"Not."

"Not yet," Aaron answers, and walks out the door.

◼▬◄ *Tabula Rasa*

By the middle of June, I am firmly ensconced at Café Louis. I take comfort in my restaurant routine. Every day except Sunday, when the restaurant is closed, I arrive at Café Louis by ten o'clock in the morning. In my Dine International life, I was working by 8 A.M. But late nights lead to late mornings.

Walking through the front door holding a pile of newspapers, I smile at the sun streaming through the windows. It reflects off Bette's chrome counter and the chrome trim of the tables. The empty dining room smells of the cleaning products the San Padre brothers use to mop the floors every night. It smells lemony.

Upturned chairs sit on the tables and their legs form a forest that I walk through to get to the counter. Grammy Jeff and Nelson are in the kitchen preparing for lunch, and I hear Grammy's music coming from the kitchen. She's a Motown kind of woman.

To the sound of the Supremes, the Temptations, and the Miracles, I brew a pot of coffee. Café Louis doesn't have and can't afford an espresso machine, so I make the coffee triple strong.

Coffeepot in hand, I take the newspapers into the kitchen, walking backward, butt first through the swinging door. At this time of day, food has yet to be grilled, fried, or sautéed. Whatever odors were in the kitchen last night have been expelled. The kitchen gets a clean slate every day.

Herby is how the kitchen smells in the morning. Every day, Grammy and Nelson cut fresh parsley, dill, and chives, infusing the air with the smell of freshness. The scent is carried on the warm breeze coming from the kitchen's screen door.

"Good morning, sugar," Grammy says.

Nelson says, "Hey, Mimi."

"Morning," I say, and make my way to the brown paper bags sitting by the door. Erlton Bakery delivers rolls every morning. Bending, I put my nose to the bags and inhale the smell of freshly baked bread. Grammy thinks this is unsanitary, and she's probably right. Which doesn't stop me from doing it. I just wait until Grammy's not looking.

Roll in hand, I situate myself on a stool in front of the metal worktable. The stool is metal and cool, which is a nice balance to the flaming hot, XXX coffee. "It'll be hot today," Grammy says. She's hot every day, no matter the temperature.

"Yes, ma'am," I say. As I drink my coffee and eat my roll, I read out loud the important parts of the *Philadelphia Inquirer*, *Philadelphia Daily News*, and South Jersey's *Courier Post*. The important parts are, of course, the gossip columns. Nelson and I laugh and Grammy sighs over the escapades of singers, actors, and people who are famous for doing nothing but getting into trouble. Of course, Café Louis has its own gossip, and I consider it my duty to keep Grammy and Nelson duly informed.

"Fly Girl got accepted to Moore College of Art," I told them yesterday. "She starts in September, which means she'll be leaving Café Louis at the end of August."

"She can't waitress and go to school?" Grammy asked.

"Please," I say. "She can barely waitress as it is."

By 11 A.M, I'm caffeinated enough to go through invoices, double-check that we received what we ordered from food and dry good suppliers, and do a fast inventory. While the lunch shift waiters set up the dining room, I take Sally on errands. We're always out of something that I forgot to order. Toilet paper, coffee filters, radishes, butter.

By the time I get back to Café Louis, lunch is half finished. I greet customers and listen to their lives, their complaints, their requests. Generally, everyone is happy with the changes I've made to the restaurant. There's grumbling at the marginal price increases, but I solve that with a smile. Or a free piece of pie.

By 3 P.M. the lunch waiters, Grammy, and Nelson have left and the San Padre brothers arrive to prepare for dinner. Me? I make another pot of XXX coffee and take it to the downstairs office. There I do very important work. Or I watch *General Hospital.*

At 4 P.M. the dinner shift waiters arrive to set up the dining room. Someone is always late, or cranky, or hungover. I sit at Bette's counter and sympathetically listen to my waiters' problems. I don't try to help them with their boyfriends, cars, or finances. I only listen. Which is enough.

This is one of my favorite parts of the day. I love watching the restaurant get dressed for dinner. Polished flatware is carefully laid on fresh napkins. Pink and blue packets are stacked next to full canisters of white sugar. Damp rags clean tables and chairs, wiping away the debris of customers past. Finally, the stage is set. The waiters will do what they've done many nights, but we approach every night as if it is a new performance.

At 4:45 P.M. the waiters, Bette, and I sit down for a staff meal. I instituted a rotating tasting of all the dishes on the menu so the waiters know what they are selling. The San Padre brothers bring out three dishes every afternoon, and the waiters descend on them like vultures. So do I. Not only is the food good, but the staff meal serves as my lunch. Sure, I could ask the San Padres to make me something at any time. But I like eating with the waiters en masse. It makes me feel like part of the family.

At 5 P.M. the senior citizens arrive. We don't have an early bird special, but we have Bette. She knows everyone's name and what they want before they order. Seats at Bette's counter are much desired, and some customers choose to wait for seats instead of being seated elsewhere.

By 6 P.M. the restaurant starts to fill. First come the Boosters. That is, families with young children who need booster seats. Next come the Homeworks, who have two working parents, neither of whom has the time or inclination to cook dinner, and kids who have homework that needs doing.

Me? I settle the paperwork from lunch. Or take a nap.

By 7:30 P.M. I'm back upstairs to help the waiters in the front of the house, or the cooks in the back of the house. The waiters don't want me to wait tables and the cooks don't want me to cook. For the waiters, I run credit cards through the machine, fill water glasses, and deliver bread baskets. For the cooks, I decipher handwriting on orders, tell waiters what dishes have to be 86'ed because we're out of ingredients, and expedite the flow of what food needs to be cooked when.

Sometimes during the night, something goes horribly wrong. A customer hates his food. The toilet overflows. The credit card machine goes off-line. There are lesser catastrophes, like a reservation not showing, or food having to be refired because it's not cooked to the customer's liking. Christopher von Hecht is used to smoothing the small bumps, but he leaves the big bumps to me. I take them head-on, but they exhaust me. What's really exhausting is having to smile. All night.

This night, the restaurant is busy. "What's the wait?" I ask Christopher, who is doing a bang-up job of manning both the door and his station.

"Five minutes."

"What is it really?"

"Twenty minutes," he says.

"I guess having a quiet dinner is out of the question." Aaron Schein has materialized at the door. He looks around at the organized chaos. "Can I help?"

"Grab an apron," Christopher says.

"We're fine," I tell Aaron. "Actually? We're great."

I wipe my hands on the white apron around my waist. "That's sexy," he says.

"The apron? Gee, do you have mother issues?"

Aaron laughs. "My mother never wore an apron. We had cooks. I lost my virginity to a cook."

"Me, too," Christopher says.

"Chrissie!" I swat a rag at him.

"What?" He moves out of rag reach. "I thought we were sharing."

"You have work to do," I tell him.

"Yeah, yeah," Christopher says. "Go tell it on the mountain."

Whatever chaos has ensued gets rehashed at the end of the night, which is 9 P.M. on weekdays and 10 P.M. on weekends. When the restaurant is cleared of its final customers, I turn on all the house lights and turn up the music to get the waiters through the drudgery of cleaning their tables and their workstations. In the kitchen, the San Padres turn on their Mexican disco to help get them through their closing work.

The waiters finish before the San Padres. As each waiter finishes, we congregate in the middle of the restaurant and chitchat about customers, ourselves, and the world. Whatever is most interesting. I cash out the waiters, exchanging real money for the tips left on credit cards. If all has gone reasonably well, both Café Louis and the waiters have made money. For the past two weeks, everyone has been happy. Including me.

* * *

Sally looks at me with sleepy headlights when I rouse her from her parking spot where she's been lolling all afternoon and night. I drive to Mom's townhouse, famished. The house is always dark, Mom already asleep. Quietly I invade the kitchen. What do I eat? A leftover-filled sandwich, of course. With mustard. Good mustard.

Saturday Night Special

At seven o'clock, the door opens. In walks a delivery man wearing a Hunter Farm T-shirt and holding three stacked boxes of produce. This guy is white; our usual delivery man is black. "Where's Eddie?" I ask the man as he hands me the delivery list to sign. His hat is pulled down over his face as he opens each box for me to quickly inspect.

"Eddie doesn't make Saturday night special deliveries," he says. "Sorry to bring this through the front door. No one answered my knock on the kitchen door. I'll carry this stuff to the kitchen."

"Sorry about the mix-up," I say. Once again, I botched the ordering. "Please tell Joe that I apologize."

"Apology accepted." The man raises his head, and hat, and I see Joe Hunter. He hoists the boxes to his shoulder and walks toward the kitchen. "Be right back."

But he doesn't come right back. Fifteen minutes later, I abandon the hostess desk, to see what Joe is doing in my kitchen. Peering through the kitchen window, I see Joe talking to the cooks. Entering through the swinging door,

I hear Joe speaking in Spanish to the San Padre brothers. "What's going on in here?"

Joe smiles and holds up a bunch of green herbs. "Lemon verbena. The newest thing in my herb house." Joe holds the lemon verbena out to me. "Smell."

Leaning forward, I put my face near Joe's hands and inhale. "Lemony."

Joe looks at my face intently. "Really good with fish."

"I bet."

"Thought you'd like to try it," Joe says. "A little present."

"Thank you."

Joe hands the bunch of herbs to Horatio, who says, *"Gracias, amigo."*

"De nada," Joe answers. Then he looks at me, and puts his hands in the front pockets of his jeans. "So. How you been?"

Glancing at the San Padre brothers, I see them grinning, looking from me to Joe. I point to the dining room. "I have to get back to work."

Joe follows me into the empty restaurant. "I can see that you're really busy."

Trying to look industrious, I walk back to the hostess desk and start rifling through the reservation book. Joe follows me. Quietly, he says, "I've been thinking about you."

I look at Joe and smile. But he doesn't say anything further. My boredom segues into frustration. I'm not interested in playing games. Aaron told me how he felt. Why can't Joe? Put up or shut up. "Thanks for the lemon verbena. I'll see you around."

"Kicking me out?" Joe asks with a smile.

"Do you want to stay? If you're hungry, you can have a seat at the counter."

Joe shakes his head. "That's why I haven't asked you out."

"What's why?"

"You're a hustle bustle. I'm a slow and steady."

I think about that for a moment, then say, "I don't get it."

"I like things to grow naturally," Joe says. "Let nature takes its course."

"Are you talking about relationships or farming?"

"Both." Joe takes off his hat and his hair flops into his face, just grazing his cheekbone. With a dirty hand, Joe tucks his hair behind his ear.

It's not that he is good-looking, I think. It's that he's earthy. Sensual.

Joe says, "I'd like to take you out. Someday. One day. Soon."

"You let me know," I tell him.

"I will." Joe smiles and heads for the door. "Good night."

"Good night."

Women

After a particularly tiring Thursday, I park Sally in front of Mom's townhouse. Looking at Sally's clock, I see that it is only 11:30 P.M. It feels like 3 A.M.

"Mimi?" Following Mom's voice, I go into the den.

Sitting on the couch are my mother and a man. I stare at the man. "Who are you?"

"Mimi, this is Sid Weiss. Dr. Sid Weiss."

"Just Sid," he says. "It's nice to meet you." Sid stands and extends his hand. He's shorter than my father, and a lot grayer. Dr. Sid is wearing olive-colored pants and a white, short-sleeved polo shirt. He speaks in a quiet, educated voice.

I shake his hand. Then we stare at each other.

"Mimi, Sid is the man I told you about? We went to the Phillies game?" She's nervous, turning all her statements into questions. "We've been spending quite a lot of time together the past few weeks?"

"Great."

Mom waves at a vase. "Sid bought me flowers, see? Aren't they beautiful?"

"Yes."

"Tulips?" Mom squeaks. "My favorite?"

Sid clears his throat. "Your mom says that you are in the restaurant business."

"Yes, I'm working at my father's restaurant. He's—" I stop.

Mom raises her eyebrows. "Sid knows your father died."

"Right." I rub my eyes. "I'm tired."

Sid stands. "If you'll excuse me, I'm going to use the restroom."

Sid walks straight to the bathroom without asking for direction. Has Sid been here before? While I've been at the restaurant?

Mom comes toward me and whispers, "I waited until you got home so I could tell you in person that I'm spending the night at Sid's. I didn't want to just leave you a note."

I stare at my mother.

She stares back at me. "You said you wanted to know where I am at all times."

"I just changed my mind."

"Mimi."

"Mommy."

"What can I say," Mom says, "to make you okay with this?"

She's not volunteering to stay home. What Mom is saying is that she's going, and she'd like to help me deal with it. But she's still going.

There's nothing Mom can say to make me okay with her spending the night with a man who isn't my father. I didn't want to know about Mom having sex with Dad. I surely don't want to know about her having sex with another man.

"Mom, you go do whatever you want to do. I'll be fine. We don't have to talk about it. Let's not get Oedipal. Anyway, Oedipus was a man. I'm a woman."

"So am I, Mimi. So am I."

●━━◖═ *Family Business, Part Two*

"The love of your life is sitting at the counter," Christopher von Hecht tells me.

"Who?" I peer out the kitchen window and see Aaron Schein.

"Chrissie, please." But Aaron looks particularly cute this evening. He's smiling.

Christopher leans over my shoulder. "He asked to see you."

Aaron smiles even wider when I come out of the kitchen. You know what? It's nice to be wanted.

"I just ordered dinner," Aaron tells me. "Will you join me?"

"I'm not hungry."

"Oh." Aaron's smile fades.

"But I'll sit with you while you eat."

"Yeah?" The smile returns. "Good." He pats the stool next to him. When I sit on the stool, next to Aaron, I catch a whiff of his cologne. Normally I don't like cologne on men. But it's something light and summery and it smells good on Aaron.

"Guess what?" he says.

"What?"

"I made a big deal today." Aaron shakes his head as if he's somewhat amazed at his success. "Can I tell you about it?"

"Sure." I expect him to chronicle the saga of the next great SHRED shopping center. Instead Aaron talks about residential development. Interrupting, I say, "I thought SHRED did commercial real estate development."

Aaron nods. "My father specializes in commercial. I've never been very interested in commercial properties. There's not a lot of room for creativity. As evidenced by almost every suburban shopping center. I worked on the commercial stuff to gain Dad's trust so he'd give me the freedom to branch into residential. Which is what happened today."

"The deal you made was with your father?"

"Yeah. It was just a handshake. But it was the biggest deal of my life." Aaron smiles. "Dad gave me permission to launch a residential division of SHRED."

"Congratulations," I say sincerely.

"Thanks." Aaron focuses his brown eyes on me. "It may sound silly to you, but I'm really excited about it."

"It doesn't sound silly to me. It sounds like an accomplishment."

Aaron blushes. How adorable is that?

"Well, Mimi Louis. You are speaking with the vice president of SHRED Residential. I am no longer a strip mall scion. Now I build homes. Quality homes for quality families. That's our motto."

Without thinking, I put my hand on his leg. "That's wonderful, Aaron."

Aaron raises his eyebrows. "See that? I'm going to tell our grandkids that you made the first move."

Removing my hand, I say, "Slow down, partner."

Aaron smiles. "When I want something, I get it."

"Do you want me or my business?"

"Both."

"I'm being serious, Aaron."

"So am I." Aaron takes my hand. "Mimi, you are going to sell SHRED the restaurant. That you are going to fall in love with me is an entirely separate matter."

"It's not a separate matter," I insist.

"But it is. Business is business. Personal is personal."

"Nay. Café Louis is my family's business."

Aaron looks serious. "To make good business decisions, I think it's best to take ego and emotion out of the equation. Not that I'm coldhearted about business. But I do separate it from the rest of my life. Work is here, play is there."

"That sounds like a nice way to live," I say. "I've never done that."

"Because you work in restaurants?" Aaron nods, answering his own question. "You work where most people go to relax."

"I guess."

"Well," Aaron says, "we'll find a new playground."

⌖ *Sisters-in-Law, Part Two*

All hail exhaustion. I fall asleep as soon as my head hits the pillow. Too soon, I am awakened by a gentle nudge. "Mimi?"

Opening my eyes, I see Allison sitting on my bed. "What's wrong?"

"Nothing, nothing. I didn't meant to startle you. I'm supposed to have breakfast with Mom. Do you know where she is?"

"She spent the night at Sid's again," I tell her. Mom's been doing that more and more.

"Oh. Wow. Wait until Jeremy hears this. Maybe I won't

tell him. He's instituted a don't ask–don't tell policy about Mom's dating."

"Can I get in on that?" Under the thin sheet, I stretch my arms and legs.

"Come on, Mimi. One of you has to be mature about Mom dating."

"Why? Hang on. Do I smell bagels?"

"They're still warm." Allison smiles. "Shall we breakfast?"

I sit at the kitchen table wearing a tank top and jammie bottoms. Allison stands in the middle of Mom's kitchen holding a brown bag and a folded section of the *Philadelphia Inquirer*. She holds the newspaper out to me and I see it's the Food section. She says, "I thought you should see that."

What I see is a big picture of Nick above a review of Il Ristorante. The *Inquirer* restaurant reviewer has given Il Ristorante a top-notch, three-star rating. I toss the paper aside. "I don't care."

"Good," Allison says. "Me, either."

I change the subject from Nick's success to my own. "Café Louis is doing really well. We're up twenty percent for the month."

"Good." Allison holds up the brown bag. "Cinnamon raisin, pumpernickel, or poppy?"

"Do you have plain?"

"No." Allison frowns. "I got the kinds we like. Mom, me and Jeremy, and the kids. I was going to take the leftover bagels home. No one in my house likes plain."

"No big deal. I'll take the unseeded half of the poppy and the unonioned half of the onion."

Allison wrinkles her brow. "But that leaves two halves that don't match."

"So?"

"Fine. Sure. Whatever you want." Allison holds the bagel bag out to me.

"No, you're right. I should have a whole one." Reaching into the bag, I find a pumpernickel bagel.

"I'm sorry," Allison says. "You like plain bagels. Now I know to get them."

I smile at her. She's such a sweetie pie. "Have we cream cheese?" I ask.

"Of course!" Allison reaches for a plastic bag. "What kind of Jewish girl would I be if I got bagels without cream cheese?"

"I've heard stories about people who eat bagels with butter."

"No. I can't believe that." Allison holds up three tubs. "Would you like plain, strawberry, or chives?"

"Plain, please. I'll put fresh chives on top."

"Oh, right. It's probably better that way. You're the food person."

Allison sits. I stand. "Fresh is best. But you know that, Ally. I bought really ripe strawberries yesterday. Why don't I slice them for you to put on your bagel?"

"No, no, the strawberry cream cheese is for the kids. I bought it out of habit."

"You're a good mom."

"I don't know about that," she says. "Speaking of

moms, how is ours? I haven't seen much of her since she started dating Sid. I miss her."

There's sadness in her voice, but when I look at Allison, she's smiling. I put a bowl of freshly cut chives on the table. "Did you tell Mom? That you'd like to spend more time with her?"

"No." Allison shakes her head vigorously. "She's enjoying herself. I don't want to get in the way of that."

While I make coffee, I make a mental note to suggest to Mom that she schedule Allison time. But how can I do that without sounding judgmental? Also, I haven't been so good at scheduling Allison time for myself.

"Mimi, how much do you think we'd get if we sold the restaurant?"

"I don't know. Why?"

"Just curious." Allison avoids looking at me by sprinkling chives on her bagel. She changes the subject. "Met any interesting men?"

"Two of them, actually." I tell Allison about Joe and Aaron.

"Joe sounds hot," she says.

"Yeah, but Aaron's probably the better choice."

"Why?"

Pouring coffee into two mugs, I say, "Aaron's a nice Jewish boy. Marriage material."

"You don't have to decide right away, do you?"

"I have to get on the marriage track." I tell Allison my mathematics equation. "How else am I going to catch up to you?"

"Me?" Allison laughs. "You don't want to catch up to me."

"But you have it all, Ally."

"Do I?"

"Yes."

Allison takes a bite of her bagel. "You're coming over tomorrow? For the barbecue? It's Father's Day."

"Is it?"

▄▄▄▄ *Family Business, Part Three*

"Do you make special deliveries to all of your customers?" Farmer Joe has once again brought boxes of produce to the restaurant. It's the middle of Saturday, a slow, hot day, and we are standing in the shade of the awning that covers the restaurant's back door.

"Your deliveries are always special," Joe says. He looks at the opened boxes, which I have inspected to make sure they match my order. "Everything here?"

I nod. "We don't need much. Tomorrow will be slow because it's Father's Day."

"Yeah." Joe leans against his truck. "Not my favorite day. Not yours, either, huh?"

"No."

"It's not even a good restaurant day," Joe says. "Mother's Day. Now that's a big business day for restaurants, and thusly for me. But Father's Day? Most people stay home and barbecue. Not good for us restaurant folk."

"No," I agree.

Joe pushes his baseball hat back on his head. "You all right, Mimi?"

"Yeah." I lean backward, against the whitewashed wall of the restaurant. "Well, no. This is the first Father's Day that I've been home. Kinda sucks."

"Where have you been?" Joe asks.

"Oh, lots of places. Most of my restaurant clients were in Europe. Paris, Rome, London, Budapest, Berlin."

Joe asks, "Do you miss traveling?"

I think for a moment. "Yeah, I do. I'm glad to be home, but I miss traveling."

"Me, too."

"You've done a lot of traveling?"

"Yep."

"Why, Farmer Joe, where have you been?"

"Let's see. All of America, Western Europe, some of Eastern Europe, bit of Canada, Mexico, a lot of South America, none of Asia, a little of Australia, Israel, Egypt, and the Rock of Gibraltar." Joe smiles.

"It must have taken you years to do all that traveling."

"Six years," Joe says. "After college, I had a job with an agricultural research firm. I went to different farms in different countries to see how American farms could adjust their methods to better compete in the international market. I did that for four years, made a lot of money, got the traveling bug, and kept going."

"You came back to take over the farm when your father died?"

"No," Joe says. "I came back long before that."

"You came back because the farm was in trouble?"

"I came back because I wanted to." Joe looks over at me.

"I guess you can't imagine someone actually wanting to be a farmer."

"It's a hard life, isn't it?"

"I love it," Joe says. "It's in my blood. My family has owned the farm for generations. My forefathers were original settlers of the area. Quakers. Welsh and British."

"My forefathers were Russian peasants."

Joe smiles. "I guess it depends which boat you got on."

"So, you worked the farm with your dad? That must have been nice."

"Not at first. Dad kept trying to get rid of me. He wanted me to be a doctor or a lawyer. I had to convince Dad that I wanted to be a farmer for myself, not for him." Joe looks over at me. "I guess you made the same choice."

"I don't know. I guess." I look at the ground.

"Hey," Joe says. I look up to see him standing in front of me. Without asking or saying anything, Joe puts his arms around my waist. He pulls me into a hug, squeezing gently. His hands go on my lower back, applying slight pressure.

Oh, does that feel good.

It feels supportive. And sexy. I close my eyes and feel his body, and I also feel safe.

And then it's over. Joe releases me and steps back, away from me. He smiles. "Looked like you needed a hug."

"I did. Thank you."

"My pleasure." Joe walks to the driver side of his truck. "I'll talk to you next week."

I nod and smile, and when Joe pulls his truck away from the restaurant, I wave.

▣▭◁ *Kings*

"Hey there, Papa Bear," I greet my brother when I find him in his backyard standing watch over the barbecue grill. "Happy Father's Day."

"Thanks," Jeremy says. "I'm glad you came. It's not an easy day, is it?"

"Why isn't there an Aunt's Day?" I ask, ignoring the point of his question. "Aunt Day. Uncle Day. In-law Day. Hallmark better get on that."

"Aunt Mimi!" The twins come tearing across the lawn. They're always so happy to see me. I love that.

"Well, if isn't Bert and Ernie," I say.

"We're not Bert and Ernie!" Gideon wraps his arms around my leg. "You know who we are, Aunt Mimi."

"Oil and vinegar?"

"No!" Ezra tackles my other leg.

"Salt and pepper?"

"Aunt Mimi!"

"Chocolate and vanilla?"

Gideon looks at Ezra. Their eyes get big as they share a thought, then scream, "Ice cream!" The boys run toward the house. "Mom? Mom! Mom!"

Oops.

"Hello, Aunt Mimi." Looking down, I see Sarah standing with her arms wrapped across her chest.

I bend to kiss Sarah's forehead. "How are you?"

From under her eyebrows, Sarah looks at me with sad,

brown eyes. For a moment, she looks exactly like my father did when he was disappointed in me. "You're forgetting me," she says.

"Of course I'm not. Why do you say that?"

"You said that because you are living here, we could spend time together. But we haven't. Not even once."

"I'm sorry, Sarah. I've been very busy at the restaurant. But I do want to spend time with you. Lots of time. When do you get out of school? End of June?"

Sarah nods.

"That's in two weeks, right? After you get out of school, we'll hang out. You and me. Okay?"

Sarah shrugs like she doesn't believe me, but wants to. She accepts my hug. Then she goes to sit with Mom.

"Where'd Sarah learn how to guilt?" I ask Jeremy.

"It's one of her innate gifts," he says. "How's Mom?"

"She sitting over there." I wave in Mom's direction. "Ask her yourself."

"Mom won't tell me the truth." Jeremy frowns. "She says I worry too much."

"You do." Peering into the grill, I say, "Might want to flip turn the meat, *jefe*."

"I don't have all of your fancy food knowledge," Jeremy says, "but I know how to barbecue. I'm a man. Barbecuing is one of my innate gifts."

"Indeed," I say. "My apologies. I shall not criticize your very manly barbecuing. At least not on Father's Day."

"Remember what we did for Father's Day when we were kids?" Jeremy asks.

Together, we say, "Chinese food."

Jeremy laughs. "People used to say, 'Your dad is a chef? You must have the best food at home.'"

"The last thing Dad wanted to do at home was cook," I say.

"We got to eat out a lot," Jeremy says. "That was fun."

"I always felt like a spy at other restaurants. Remember how Dad would grill us about the food we ate? 'Too sweet? Too salty? Too sour? Too bitter?' We had to make sure Café Louis's food was better than any other restaurants."

"Remember Mitsitam Restaurant in Westfield?" Jeremy asks.

"Of course," I say. "Dad thought the Mitsitam was our biggest competitor."

"A few years ago, a shopping center went up across the street from the Mitsitam," Jeremy says. "That center has a Friendly's, Boston Market, and a Subway."

"Oy."

"Not surprisingly, the Mitsitam closed." Jeremy nods in silent homage to the Mitsitam. "Anyway, when I was going through Dad's invoices and paperwork, I found a copy of a letter he wrote the Mitsitams saying that they were welcome to eat at Café Louis any time. Free of charge."

"Really?"

"Yep," Jeremy says. "I asked Bette and she confirmed it. She also said that the Mitsitams never came to Café Louis, as far she knew. They moved to Oklahoma, I think."

"Still," I say.

"Absolutely," Jeremy agrees. "Would you ask my darling wife to bring her buns out here? And the mustard and ketchup and relish."

▰▰▰ *Sisters-in-Law, Part Three*

Allison is standing at the kitchen's island, mustard jar in hand, staring at a potted plant.

"Ally?"

She doesn't move or break her gaze.

"Ally? Allison? Major Tom?"

She shakes her head and turns to me. "Sorry. What's up?"

"Jeremy's ready for the rolls and condiments. Are you okay?"

"Tired. I'm tired." She rubs her eyes. "I think I fell asleep standing still with my eyes open. It was just so quiet in here. There's always so much noise in the house. It's so loud, so often. With everyone outside and Mom and Jeremy looking after the kids, I had an unexpected moment of peace." Allison looks at me. "Do you know what I mean?"

"Sort of." I pull the twist tie from a bag of buns and start to pile them on a plate. "The restaurant gets very frantic around lunch and dinner, but before and after that, the place is nice and quiet. But too much quiet in the house? Not a good thing."

Allison nods. "Are you making a profit yet?"

"A little. But I have until the end of the summer. I have time."

"Right." Allison hands me another bag of rolls. "You have time."

A noise I recognize as Mom's cell phone rings through the kitchen. Mom's cell is on the kitchen table next to her purse. I look at the caller ID. "It's Sid."

Allison says, "Aren't you going to take the phone to Mom?"

"He'll leave a message."

"Mimi."

"What? Mom's hanging out with her grandkids, and kids, which she hasn't done in some time. Today is a family day. Sid can wait."

Allison shakes her head. "You and your brother are being really immature about this. Why am I the only one who's thinking about what's best for Mom?"

"Because you're the only adult among us. Or hadn't you noticed?"

Quietly, Allison says, "I noticed."

"Seriously, Ally. You're supermom. Why are we having a barbecue for Jeremy? This day and every day should be about you."

Allison hands me a platter with the rolls and condiments. She puts Mom's cell on the platter. "Give that to your mother."

"Aren't you coming outside to eat?"

Allison rubs her eyes again. "I have to put laundry in the dryer."

"You're doing laundry? Now?"

"Mimi, I'm always doing laundry."

◼️═🍴 *Canapé*

"Café Louis. This is Mimi. How can I help you?"

"You can have dinner with me tonight. An official first date."

"Who is this?"

"Aaron Schein." A beat later he says, "Who else would it be?"

"No one. I'm kidding. I knew it was you. Did you say dinner?"

I wait for Aaron near the hostess desk wearing the khaki capri pants and a pink halter top I wore to work. My pink and silver bead bracelet is on my wrist and a matching necklace is around my neck.

Christopher von Hecht appears at the hostess desk. "Do you want some advice?"

"No," I say.

"Canapé," he says.

"Excuse me?"

"On first dates, you should canapé. Be delicious, but not filling. A tasty hors d'oeuvre that whets the appetite for the meal. A gastronomic prelude, if you will."

Canapé certainly sounds feminine and flirty. Maybe Christopher von Hecht is right. But I'm not going to tell him that. "Chrissie, please. Go yenta somewhere else."

◖▭▬◗ *USA Steaks*

Peach? Apricot? I'm trying to name the color of Aaron's shirt. Whatever color it is, the shirt is well made. Custom made? Maybe. His orangey shirt goes nicely with the blueberry and celery print on his tie. Silk tie, looks like. The loafers are alligator. And Gucci. I know my reptiles, and Italians. Aaron's ensemble is good. The boy knows how to dress.

Aaron looks at me looking at him. "Are you checking me out?"

"And if I am?"

"I came from a meeting," Aaron says. "Otherwise, I'd have changed into more casual clothes."

"You look very nice."

"Thank you, Mimi. So do you."

"Thank you. I'm glad we're doing this. Having a date."

Aaron smiles. "Yeah?"

"Yeah."

See? I can canapé.

"Are you kidding me?" I ask. Aaron has pulled his yellow Hummer into a parking lot. I see a crowd of people waiting outside a building that looks like a ranch house. On top of the ranch restaurant is a glowing orange sign. USA Steaks.

"What? This place has great food." Aaron gets out of the Hummer. He walks around the car to my side and opens my door.

Well, I am a filet mignon. Am I not?

As we approach the door, I say, "It looks like there's a two-hour wait."

Aaron smiles and walks to the hostess desk. The hostess coos, "Hi, Aaron. How are you this evening? Table for two?"

We're seated immediately.

"Let me guess," I guess. "Your family owns this joint?"

"Yep. Want to meet the chef? I think there are four chefs. I can introduce you."

"No. Thanks." Looking at the enormous menu, I search for the smallest steak and order it with a glass of Cabernet Sauvignon. Aaron orders the largest steak, French fries, and string beans. "And a Coors Light," he finishes.

When the food comes, Aaron reaches for the salt and pepper, which he liberally applies to his beans and fries. "You haven't tasted it yet," I say.

"What?"

"How do you know the food needs seasoning if you haven't tasted it?" I ask.

"It's not seasoning," he says. "It's salt and pepper." When he's done with the salt and pepper, Aaron reaches for the A1 Steak Sauce.

"You can't use that," I tell him.

Confused, Aaron looks at the label. "Why not?"

"If a steak is cooked to perfection, it has its own juices and doesn't need to be suffocated with sauce."

Aaron points at my plate. "You eat your steak the way you like, and I'll eat mine the way I like. Okay?"

"Okay," I say with a sigh. "But you're doing it wrong."
Aaron laughs.

Aaron eats with gusto. He cuts a piece of meat, puts it on his fork, spears a French fry or string bean, and puts the whole thing in his mouth. He chews rhythmically, his head bobbing slightly. When he has swallowed, Aaron takes a swig of beer, then starts the whole process over again. Piece of meat, French fry, string bean. Chew, swallow, swig. And again. And again.

I find this fascinating.

Long have I believed that men eat the same way they screw. A man who shovels food into his mouth is not interested in taste or texture. A man who eats the same things all the time is not interested in variety. A man who gets up from the table before the woman has finished eating? Please. I want a man who smells his vegetables, savors his meat, and plays with his potatoes.

Aaron is eating quickly, but he looks to be enjoying his food. His eating method does not fit into any of my categories. I don't know what to do about that.

Soft, Gentle, Nice

Aaron drives me back to Café Louis. "I have to go inside and finish the night," I tell him.

"Should I walk you to the door, or would you like to be kissed in the car?"

Turning in my seat, I look at Aaron. The date was perfectly fine, but I'm not overcome with desire for Aaron. I like that he enjoys life. And food. And clothes. Aaron appreciates the finer things in life. So what is he doing with me? Good question. I ask it. "Why are you pursuing me? You could have any woman you want."

"Here's the thing." Aaron looks serious. "I've dated a lot of women and it always turns out the same way. They start out saying my family's money doesn't matter, but in time, they forget about me, the person, and only see the lifestyle. Then I lose respect for them and start treating them badly. But they put up with it, because they think it'll pay off in the end. You, Mimi, don't let me get away with anything. You are independent, smart, and successful in your own right. That's incredibly attractive to me, as is the fact that you aren't falling all over me. And you have a great ass."

"You'll hold that against me later."

Aaron smiles. "Your ass?"

"No. Way no," I say. "The things you said about me. Independent, smart, successful. You'll learn to hate those things."

Aaron is quiet for a few moments. Then, "I don't get it."

"It's like this." I turn to face him. "Right now you like my independence because it poses a challenge for you. But you'll come to resent it."

"Before we get to the resentment, may I kiss you?"

"Might as well do it now," I say, "before we break up."

His lips are smooth, and warm. Soft. Gentle. Nice.

◼━◁ *Falling*

"And that's how the date ended," I tell Madeline. "With a nice kiss."

We are shopping for kitchen gadgets at Fante's on Ninth Street, in Philadelphia's Italian Market. I buy equipment from the much cheaper Trenton China and Pottery store, but Madeline wants only top-of-the-line stuff. Sieves, peelers, mandolins. She shops for kitchen gadgets the way other women shop for shoes.

"This is the good-on-paper predicament right?" Madeline squeezes down an aisle. "I'm bored already. You'll never fall for this guy."

"What good is falling? Falling is a bad thing. It hurts. It leaves bruises. And if you fall hard enough, it takes a while to get back on your feet."

"What if someone catches you?" Madeline asks.

"For me to fall in love, I'd have to trust that someone is going to catch me. Right now I'm not big on trusting men. I'm definitely not ready to have sex. So maybe I don't want to fall in love. Maybe I want to stand upright and walk into love. Or at least glide. That's it, Maddie. I'll glide into a relationship with Aaron. I should. He's a nice person."

"What's nice got to do with it? There's either chemistry or there isn't." Madeline tosses a chocolate mold into her basket. "Speaking of which, what's up with Farmer Joe?"

"I haven't heard from him. He has yet to ask me out for a date."

"Call him."

"No. No. Oh, and? No."

"Excuse me," Madeline says. "What millennium is this?"

"If Joe wants me, he knows where to find me. Look at Aaron. He's pursuing me. It's nice. It's good for my battered ego."

"Batter." Madeline reaches for a wooden spoon. "Thanks for reminding me."

Specials

"You hungry?" Nelson asks me when I walk into the kitchen in the late afternoon.

"A little." Nelson is wearing a Sean John baseball hat and a T-shirt with Malcom X's picture. What would Brother Malcolm think of Brother Diddy? What does Nelson think of them? I don't know.

"Let me make you something." Nelson reaches for his chef coat.

"You don't have to, Nellie. You worked all day."

"I want to." Nelson smiles at me. "You worked with famous chefs, right? How about I cook you one of my specialties and you tell me what you think."

Twenty minutes later, Nelson brings me a plate holding peanut-crusted tuna, sautéed spinach, and white rice spiked with corn, diced tomato, and cilantro. "Wow," I say.

Chewing, I look at Nelson with surprise. "You got game."

Nelson smiles broadly. "It's good?"

"Yes." I put more food in my mouth. With real delight, Nelson watches me eat. Mouth full, I ask, "Where did you learn to cook like this?"

"Grammy Jeff taught me a lot, but she doesn't know formal cooking. I read a lot of cookbooks. I watch cooking shows on TV. Then I try stuff here or at home."

"You like cooking?" I ask. I thought this was only a job to him.

"Yeah," Nelson says. "I guess it runs in the family."

"Nelson, you have talent."

"Thank you." Nelson hangs his head to hide his grin. "I thought about going to culinary school, but I can't afford it."

When I finally put my fork down, I say, "You should do the daily specials."

Nelson frowns. "We don't do daily specials here."

"We do now."

⬤▬◖ *Mom AWOL*

At the end of the night, Christopher von Hecht sits across from me in the office while I count money. "You can go home," I tell him.

"I'm waiting," Christopher says.

"For what?"

"For you to tell me about your first of many dates with Aaron Schein."

"Oh. Why do I have to tell you?"

"You have to tell me so I can tell everyone else."

Christopher rolls his eyes. "Come on, kiwi. You know there are no secrets in restaurants."

"It was very nice. Ended with a kiss. A nice kiss."

"Ah, isn't that sweet?" Christopher claps. "Can I be a bridesmaid?"

"Chrissie, stop."

"Look at you, dating a nice Jewish boy. Your mother must be thrilled."

It's then that I realize I haven't told Mom about Aaron. I haven't seen her for days. Mom's been spending almost all of her time with Sid.

She's not home when I get there. I could call Mom's cell, but it's almost midnight and she's probably asleep. And if she isn't asleep, I don't want to know why not.

I leave a note on Mom's bed. "Mom—Let's have lunch or dinner. Come to the restaurant.—Mimi." She's gotta eat and she's gotta come home. Eventually.

◖▬◗ *Awakening the Diva*

The summer slump begins the first week of July. Everyone who can afford to goes to the Jersey shore. On the first Saturday of July, business slows to a crawl. The waiters gossip and groan about the lack of tippage. When the phone rings, I jump at it and pray for a reservation.

"Café Louis. This is Mimi. How can I help you?"

"This is Joe Hunter."

Just the sound of his voice gives me tingles. "Hello, Joe. How are you?"

"Well, Mimi. I think it's time."

"For?"

"Us to get together."

"Yeah?" Flip flop goes my tummy.

"What are you doing for the Fourth of July?" Joe asks.

"I don't know."

"Well, Fourth of July is the only day during the summer that I let everyone on the farm take off. I'm going to my family's house down the shore. Would you like to come with me?"

"That all depends," I say. "What shore?"

"LBI," Joe answers. That's Jersey-speak for Long Beach Island.

I haven't been to LBI since I was in high school. We spent our annual family vacations there. At the end of August, Dad closed the restaurant and rented a house for a week. Mom preferred the more urbane town of Margate, but my father loved rustic LBI.

No man is an island, he'd say, except the Isle of Man.

"I'd love to go with you," I tell Joe.

"I'm driving to Hunter Farm and Joe is driving to the shore from there," I tell Madeline over the phone.

"What about Aaron?"

"I haven't made a commitment to Aaron. Joe asked me out and there's nothing wrong with going."

Madeline says, "Get your sexual energy out with Joe so you can take things slowly with Aaron."

"Maddie, I'm not sleeping with Joe."

"Fine. But your sexuality is a precious thing. Maybe it's time to rouse your diva."

I am not going to sleep with Joe. But I decide to go for a WASAP. "I need a waxing as soon as possible," I beg the receptionist at The Make-Up Bar.

"Weren't you just here?" Lisa smiles as she whisks hair from my upper lip.

"I have a date. Of sorts. I want to look good for him."

"You should look good for yourself," Lisa said.

"Can you give me a bikini wax? Just in case."

Later that afternoon, standing in the shower, looking down at my body, I think about the diva. I miss her.

I rummage through Olga the Suitcase looking for CDs I haven't yet unpacked. Aha! There she is. The diva's diva. Madonna. *The Immaculate Collection.*

In the living room, I put the CD in Mom's player. As Madonna sings, I dance around the living room in my bra and panties. My damp hair showers droplets of water as I dance to three songs. Then I run my hands through my hair and smile.

I'm back, the diva says.

☞ *The Diva Smiles*

"Hello?" Nobody answers my call into the Hunter house. "Mrs. Hunter? Joe?" Walking through the house toward the back door, I look for signs of life. Nobody's home, but a wet towel hanging on a line in the backyard tells me that someone has recently showered. Joe? Here's hoping.

A trail of droplets turning to mud leads me to one of the barns. "Joe?"

"In here," he says in hushed tones. Following his voice, I enter the barn and pause to let my eyes adjust to the darkness. In the slanted light, I see Joe lying on his belly, peering under a barrel that sits on two other stacks. Joe is wearing jeans but no shirt. His back is quite pale, his arms tan, and everything is long and muscular. "Hi," Joe whispers. "Come here."

I approach slowly. Joe points under the barrel. "Look," he says. I can't see what he's pointing at, so I crouch to a squat. Still, I can't see under the barrel. So I lie down on my stomach on the wooden floor. Leaning on my elbows, I follow Joe's gaze.

Several feet away, nestled on an old blanket, lies a dog. Five newborn puppies squirm at her belly. The dog's eyes are half shut, as if she's exhausted and happy.

"She gave birth yesterday," Joe whispers.

"She's your dog?"

"She wandered onto the farm without a collar. I gave her a home."

The dog mamma opens her eyes and starts to lick one of the puppies while another pup sucks at her teats. "It's beautiful, isn't it?" Joe smiles at me. His hair is damp and I can smell his minty shampoo.

"You showered," I say.

"I do that from time to time." Joe moves his head, and I see the lines around his brown eyes. He sits up and I see brown hair on his chest. The hair forms a single, darker line as it marches down his belly and into his jeans.

When I return my eyes to Joe's face, his eyebrows are raised. "What are you looking at?" he asks.

"Nothing." Embarrassed, I put my hands on the floor and sit, preparing to stand.

"Wait." In a quick movement, Joe swings around his legs and sits facing me. My head comes to his armpit and I see dark brown hair there. It has been quite a while since I've seen a male body. I miss it.

"Mimi, can I kiss you?"

I nod.

Joe leans forward, closes his eyes, and touches his lips to mine. His mouth is firm, but not hard. He starts lightly, then presses more purposefully. I feel one of Joe's chapped hands on my cheek, then it moves into my hair and Joe moves my head, angling it so that he can put his tongue in my mouth. With his other hand, Joe moves me so that my head falls into the crook of his elbow, my body leaning against his bent legs.

Joe showered, but didn't shave. His stubble is rough against my face. The roughness of his beard contrasts with the softness of his tongue. I like it. It's a texture thing.

The diva smiles.

We kiss for what seems like a long time. It's dark. It's cool. It's quiet. Joe isn't in a hurry. He's not pressuring me. Slowly, I feel my body relax. My shoulders separate and lean against Joe's legs. My head rests on his bent knees.

Feeling my relaxation, Joe moves his hand from my back to my hip, then slowly to my outer thigh, then more slowly to my inner thigh. He's giving me every opportunity to stop him. I don't. Joe pushes his thumb into my inner thigh, massaging it. A simple thing, but it feels so good that I moan.

Joe moves backward, lying on the wood floor, and pulls me on top of him. He moves me up his body until we are face-to-face and kissing. How nice that he didn't climb on top of me. Yes, all my weight is on him, but I don't feel self-conscious about that. Rather, because I'm on top, I feel in control of the situation. That makes me more relaxed.

Joe wraps his arms around my waist and raises my shirt just enough to put his hands on the small of my back. Gently but firmly, Joe massages the small of my back. I moan again and put my face into Joe's neck. After a few minutes, Joe puts his hands on my hips and lowers me so that we are crotch to crotch. My hips start to grind.

Yes, the diva says.

My brain starts to work. How far should I take this? Answer: no farther. This way lies trouble. I don't want to start another relationship with sex. My hips grind to a halt.

Joe rolls me onto my back and hovers over me, kneeling on an elbow. He smiles. I want to say something. Like, "I don't want to start a relationship this way." Or, "Although I'm very close to ripping your jeans off, I'm not ready to get naked with you." Or, "I'm sure you could make me scream in a thousand different ways, but before I lose all rational thought, I think we should stop."

Instead I push him away gently and say, "Okay?"

"Okay," Joe says. He kisses me again, leans his body

onto mine, and runs his hand from the inside of my armpit past my breast, down my hip to my thigh.

The diva shouts, Please!

Wrapping my arm around his neck, I push Joe's mouth onto mine. I move his hand inside my shorts. His fingers touch me, rough against the soft cotton of my panties.

Yes! the diva screams.

"I thought you wanted to stop." Joe's breathing nears a pant.

"What?"

The diva says, Don't stop.

"We should stop," I say.

"Okay." Joe rolls onto his back. "Okay."

We lie next to each other, looking at the ceiling of the barn.

The diva pouts.

◼▬▬◧ *Driving Down the Shore*

Ten minutes later, I'm in Joe's red pickup truck. It's a tricked-out pickup, with white leather seats and immaculate floor mats.

Joe settles behind the driver's seat and folds up his sleeves. He's put on a long-sleeved, button-down shirt, the white cotton so worn that it's almost transparent. The unbuttoned shirt hangs open, like a gauze curtain displaying Joe's chest. "Be right back."

Joe returns carrying a guitar case, which he deposits in the back of the truck. "You play guitar?" I ask.

Joe turns the ignition. "I was in a band in college."

"Where did you go to college?" Nice segue, I congratulate myself.

"Cornell." Joe turns, looking for something behind the seat. "Be right back."

Cornell, huh? There's more to Farmer Joe than I thought.

When he returns, Joe puts a white bag of cider donuts on my lap. "Mom made these yesterday, before she left to visit my cousins for a week."

"I haven't had cider donuts since I was a kid," I say. "Oh, the memories."

When Joe finally peels the truck out of the driveway, dirt and gravel crunch under the truck's wheels. As we drive from the farm to the highway, the breeze billows Joe's shirt away from his torso and my hair blows around my head.

Soon we are in stop-and-go traffic on the densely commercialized highway Route 70. I eat a cider donut while Joe drums his fingers against the steering wheel. This part of shore driving sucks.

Finally, Route 70 turns from a strip mall hell into a two-lane highway. We drive into Burlington County and through the town of Medford, traveling backward in Jersey time as the road becomes more rural and less developed. Family-owned lawn care centers and lumber yards stretch out on either side of the road, separated by miles of trees and grass.

In Southampton, I see a farm silo, and within minutes,

farm stands dot the road offering berries, melons, and early tomatoes.

A small sign announces that we are in Woodland Township, and soon we come to a traffic circle that will put us on Route 616 and take us to LBI. As we turn around the circle, I see Billy Boy's Four Mile Tavern, a ramshackle bar that looks like it belongs in the Old West. Milling in front of Billy Boy's are men wearing trucker hats, jeans, and brown leather belts with silver buckles that glint with sunshine. Their trucks sit in the dirt parking lot, lined up like horses resting. To my surprise, Joe pulls into the parking lot. "Do you want to use the bathroom?" he says.

"No," I say quickly.

"Are you sure? It's another hour to LBI. Speak now, or forever hold your pee."

"I'll be fine," I say.

"Suit yourself," Joe says. He leaves me in the parking lot.

I sit in the truck and start to wonder what I'm doing here, in the middle of nowhere, with a man I barely know. I think about the woman who worked for Dine International, and she seems like someone else, a different version of me. What if I hadn't walked in on Nick and tongue ring girl? I would've gone on my merry way, living and working with Nick, expecting an engagement ring and planning our future. Do I still want the same things I wanted? Husband? Children? Home?

I think about Joe's body, his jeans, the feel of his hands

on my body. Get your mind out of the barn, Mimi. Be practical. If I want the husband-children-home dream, I have a much better shot at it with Aaron than Joe.

But what would life with Joe Hunter be like? Could I be a farmer's wife? Or even a farmer's girlfriend? Does it matter what he does, as long as he's a good person? Joe is well educated, well traveled and well hung. What more could a girl want?

Joe gets back into the truck and turns on the CD player. Springsteen, of course. We turn onto Route 616 and cross into the Pine Barrens, Jersey's wonderland of protected forest and wetland. I close my eyes and let the music and fresh air wash over me.

Beach Haven

It's late afternoon when we emerge from the Pine Barrens and cross the two long bridges onto Long Beach Island. The bay is filled with boats of all sizes and engine power. Seagulls squawk overhead. From the top of the second bridge, I look across the bay and see the sky looks rather dark. Looking to my left, I see the Dutchman Bauhaus, a behemoth of a restaurant that looms over the bay. Seeing the Dutchman brings back memories.

At a busy intersection, we turn right onto Long Beach Boulevard and drive through Ship Bottom. The boulevard is stacked with shops and restaurants. Parents and children, boyfriends and girlfriends, and packs of teenagers roam the sidewalks. Everyone is dressed very casually, in shorts, T-shirts, and sneakers or flip-flops. On LBI, there's an unwritten no posing rule.

As Long Beach Boulevard turns into Bay Avenue, we enter the town of Beach Haven. The street becomes less dense as development bends to the nature of the island. Bay Avenue narrows and the beach takes over one side of the street. Steep wooden steps lead to the dunes. Looking at the sand, I realize that I have been away from the Jersey shore for far too long.

Turning onto West Avenue, Joe comes to a stop in front of a single Cape house with beige clapboard siding and a roof blackened by the salt, sun, and rain.

"This is it," Joe says. He looks fondly at the house. "Dad bought it in 1962, just as the island was getting developed. I keep meaning to fix it up, but I kind of like it the way it is. It's not fancy, but almost everything is the same as it was when I was a kid."

I say, "I have to pee."

Hustling my bladder up the brick path leading to the front door, I see that the front lawn is filled with stones, pebbles, and shells, bringing the beach to the house. Inside, Joe points straight ahead to the bathroom. Ten steps takes me through the living room, which has a red and blue plaid couch and several wicker and rattan chairs with blue and red cushions. A glass-topped, white wicker coffee table stands in the middle of the room. It's basic beach decor. Nothing fancy.

As I sit on the toilet and gratefully pee, I look around the bathroom. The tub and sink are white, the tiled floor is white, and the walls are sky blue. It's clean and functional.

"Feel better?" Joe asks as I walk into the kitchen.

"Much," I answer. The kitchen walls are pale yellow, the floor is white linoleum, and the cabinets are painted white. The appliances are cute and retro, until I realize that they are the original refrigerator and stove. There's no dishwasher in sight. But I do see a French press coffee maker, next to which sits a Ziploc bag of finely ground coffee beans. Gottta love a man who knows the value of a good grind.

Joe sticks his torso out of the refrigerator. He smiles and holds up a bag of blueberries. "Breakfast," he says.

"Breakfast?"

"Yeah," Joe says. "I have strawberries if you prefer them."

"Wait. You didn't say anything about spending the night here."

Joe takes his head out of the refrigerator. He looks surprised. "I thought you understood that. It's already late afternoon and we just got here. But, it's no big deal. I should have clarified. We'll drive back tonight." He turns back to the refrigerator.

I don't want to ruin Joe's Fourth fun. Should I stay here? Walking through the rest of the house, I find two bedrooms downstairs, one with a king-sized bed and the other with a day bed and a queen-sized bed.

The diva stirs.

"There are four more beds upstairs," Joe says as he comes up behind me in the master bedroom. "I'm not trying to pressure you, but the house has plenty of beds. If you don't want to sleep in mine."

Turning to face Joe, I say, "I'm tempted."

"To sleep here or sleep with me?" He smiles and takes a step closer to me.

The diva whispers, Stay.

"I'll stay," I tell Joe. "Upstairs. You stay downstairs. Agreed?"

"Agreed."

◼━◗ *Young Man and the Sea*

Joe wants to swim in the ocean. He's like a little kid. "Come on, come on," he says as I grab sunscreen and a towel on which to sit. I have no intention of going in the ocean. If I go in, I have to shower and redo myself. I didn't bring hair products or cosmetics. Is a swim in the ocean worth the effort? I think not.

At the water's edge we stand, me in my khaki shorts and burnt orange tank top, Joe in long, navy swimming trunks and a green T-shirt with white lettering that reads "Hunter Farm, Westfield, NJ."

"I love it," Joe says as we stand on the beach, staring at the ocean. It's after five o'clock and most people are packing up their chairs, blankets, umbrellas, and kids, and heading home. Oblivious to the commotion around him, Joe stares at the white waves and says, "If the earth is female, the ocean is male. To farm the earth, you have to nurture it. But to swim in the ocean, you have to fight it."

"That's poetic," I say. "Who wrote that?"

Still looking at the ocean, Joe smiles. "I did."

Peeling off his T-shirt, Joe hands it to me like I'm a towel girl in his corner of the boxing ring. His long, muscled torso looks capable of anything. Joe strides through the shallow water until he is waist high in the ocean. Then he swims. Long, smooth strides take him out, then farther out, farther, then too far for my comfort. I look around for a lifeguard, but they have already called it a day. Squinting at the horizon, I see that Joe has stopped swimming. Facing east, his back to the shore, Joe raise his arms above the water, fists clenched. What the heck is he doing?

His head tilts back and it looks like he is saying something, but I can't hear him over the roar of the ocean. He punches the air with one fist, and I realize that he is shouting something. Something no one else can hear. Something between Joe and the ocean.

Surrounded by earth for most of his days, maybe Joe finds God in the ocean. Maybe he's mad at God. Maybe God has some explaining to do. On the other hand, Joe could be thanking God for his gifts. What is Joe saying? I won't ask. It's between them.

When Joe steps out of the ocean, I hand him a beach towel. "Feel better?" I ask.

"Much," he says, smiling. He kisses me, leaving salt on my mouth.

◼━◱ Jersey Girl

We walk up the dune, down the dune, and back onto Bay Avenue. As we cross the street, Joe takes my hand. That makes me smile.

We walk from the ocean to the bay, which is only a few blocks. West Avenue opens into a cul de sac that hosts a small marina and several restaurants whose verandas are open and waiting for island diners. But it's that in-between hour, when people are home showering sand from their bodies, having a cocktail, deciding where to dine. The absence of people makes the marina temporarily quiet, and moody. Boats are tied to ancient-looking driftwood poles that poke out of the bay at various heights. The boats are bobbing dutifully in rhythm with the soft lapping of the water against the dock. Nearby stands a red-roofed bait and tackle shack with a white box marked "Ice" in orange letters.

Joe leads me onto the walkway overlooking the bay. We stand and look at nothing. No boats pass, no fish leap. There's nothing but water, and I become hypnotized by the movement of the blue-gray peaks. Joe puts his hand on my shoulder, near my neck. The simple pressure and warmth of his hand makes my neck muscles relax. Closing my eyes, I lean against him. Then a raindrop hits me square in the face.

"Uh oh," Joe says. We run.

* * *

An hour later, it's still raining. From the shelter of Chez Hunter's covered back patio, I watch the rain while Joe cooks burgers on an old but clean grill. We eat quietly, in the light of citronella candles. When the rain stops, Joe suggests returning to the beach. "It's going to be wet," I say. Joe smirks and gets me a pair of swimming trunks, which are huge but tie at my waist, and a green sweatshirt that says "Hunter Farm." We go to the beach carrying two chairs and a cooler of beer.

We sit on a blanket, drink beer, and watch the ocean. Then Joe says, "I'm going to get my guitar." He leaves me on the beach in the dark.

When he comes loping across the sand with his guitar on his back, neck pointing downward and the strap across his bare chest, Joe looks like a Jersey cowboy drunk on corn and tomatoes.

The diva rises.

After tuning the guitar, Joe strums, then sings the first words of "Jersey Girl."

"I haven't heard this song in a long time," I say. But I remember the words. I sha-la-la through the chorus with Joe. The sha-la-laing goes on for a while, until I tell Joe, "I have to pee."

He points at the ocean.

"Nay," I say.

We pack up and head back to Chez Hunter. I dance across the sand. When we get to the top of the dune, I close my eyes, spread my arms wide, and shout, "I'm a Jersey girl!" And then of course I fall.

First, I tilt. Unable to right myself, I stumble in the sand. As I'm about to do a header down the dune, Joe throws his arm around my waist and puts me onto my feet. "Guess I've had a little more to drink than I thought," I say as Joe laughs at me.

When I come out of Chez Hunter's bathroom, Joe is leaning against the wall with his hands in his jean pockets, his white shirt open and blowing in the breeze. I walk to Joe and put my hands on his chest, leaning against him. His skin is warm, his chest hair soft. Turning my chin up, I give Joe my mouth and he kisses me, wrapping his arms around my shoulders.

The diva shudders.

Pulling away from Joe's body, I say, "I'm getting a little tipsy, so let me tell you now that, contrary to what I may say or do in the next few hours, I don't want to have sex with you tonight. It would be great if one of us could remember that."

Joe smiles.

When Joe comes out of the bathroom, I'm sitting on the couch. Sitting might be an overstatement. I'm propped up on the couch and trying not to look drunk. "Sing me another song," I say to Joe. Or that's what I mean to say. It comes out kind of slurred.

Joe sits across from me, on the coffee table next to the couch, holding the neck of his guitar. "Falling asleep?"

"No. No, Joe. Joe? You have a great voice. Sexy. Very sexy."

"Yeah?" he asks, as if he doesn't know that. Joe takes off his shirt, spreads his legs, and puts the guitar on his knee.

Zounds! the diva shouts.

"Do you know the song 'If I Needed You'?" Joe asks as he tunes his guitar.

"Yes." I don't.

Who cares? the diva says. I want him.

◼️═🍴 *The Morning After*

Naked is how I wake up. Did we . . . ?

I wish, the diva mumbles.

Sun streaming through the dormer windows tells me that I am in an upstairs bedroom and it's at least mid-morning. Putting two feet on the floor, I see my clothes in a heap near the bed. I remember stripping and diving under the covers. Alone.

There's a shower in the upstairs bathroom, but I don't have a change of clothes, or underwear, so why bother bathing? I put my clothes on and root around in my bag for a piece of gum in lieu of a toothbrush. Aha! Chiclet.

Quietly, in case Joe is still sleeping, I step down the stairs. His bedroom door is open, the bed made, the room tidied. Walking through the living room, I see Joe sitting at the kitchen table. Plastic containers are on the table, emptied of their berries. The French press holds what looks like cold coffee. On the counter is a small carton of orange juice. A newspaper is spread out in front of Joe. He's been up, and out.

"Good morning," I say, walking toward the kitchen, and toward Joe to deliver a Chiclet-clean kiss.

" 'Morning." Joe stands up and his chair scrapes against the linoleum, making a loud, abrupt squeak. Joe walks to the sink. Back turned to me, he says, "I didn't know when you'd wake up."

Okay. Not the greeting I expected. Looking at the kitchen clock, I see that it is almost eleven, which is an average Sunday wake-up time. Maybe not for farmers. "You could have woken me," I say.

Turning to the kitchen table, Joe gathers the newspaper, cup, and carton. "We should probably get going."

Awkward is in the air. Why? Is it something I did? Or what I didn't do?

"I'll get my bag," I say.

When I come back downstairs, Joe asks, "Do you want some of the *Times*?" He points to the refolded *New York Times* sitting on the kitchen table.

"Sure." I leaf through the stack. "I'll take Travel, Style, and the magazine. I just want the fun parts."

Joe nods, as if reading more into my statement than I intended.

In the truck, my tummy rumbles. We pass Fritz's Bakery, Chicken or Egg restaurant, and Uncle Bill's Pancake House. But Joe has already eaten. Can I make it home without food? Nope. Seeing a Wawa convenience store sign ahead, I ask Joe to stop and he does.

"Do you want anything?" I ask. He doesn't.

When I return, Joe looks at my twenty-four ounce cup of coffee and laughs. I say, "I need massive doses of caffeine in the morning." I also need food in the morning. I bought a Wawa sausage, cheese, and egg sandwich, hoping the fat and carbs will soak up the vestiges of beer in my body. While Joe navigates an intersection, I take three big bites of the sandwich. When the truck is safely turned and merged, Joe looks at me.

"Why are you eating that?" he asks.

"I'm hungry," I answer with my mouth full.

"I was going stop for breakfast," Joe says.

I stop chewing. "Oh. I thought you'd already eaten. We can still stop. Let's stop." I put the sandwich back in its wrapper.

"No, it's fine."

"You're hungry," I tell him.

"I'll be fine."

"Eat the rest of this." I push the sandwich at him. "Then we can stop for an early lunch. Okay?"

"I'm fine, thanks." He smiles. Finally.

"I insist," I insist.

"Mimi, I don't want to eat that."

"Sure you do," I tell him, and unwrap the sandwich. Unfastening my seat belt, I scoot across the bench until my leg touches Joe's. "Hi."

He looks down at me. "Hi."

Dancing the half-eaten sandwich in front of Joe's face, I speak in the high, squeaky voice that makes my nephews laugh. "Eat me, eat me."

Joe raises an eyebrow. "I would . . ."

136

But I don't let him finish the sentence. I cram the sandwich into his mouth and move back to my seat, fastening
my seat belt. Joe laughs.

Back at the farm, Joe walks me to my car. I'm not sure how
to take my leave. Tossing my bag in the car, I turn to him.
"I had a great time."

"Good," he answers. He looks at the ground.

"Did you?" I'm not sure and I want to know.

He thinks for a moment. "I guess I'm confused."

"About?"

"What you want." Joe puts his hands in the pockets of
his jeans. "In the barn. On the couch last night."

Couch? I don't remember the couch.

Joe says, "You start. Then you stop."

I stopped. Good for me. Bad for Joe. I say, "What happened to letting things develop naturally?"

Joe says, "Making love to you would be the most natural thing in the world."

That makes me—and the diva—smile.

But wait just a minute. "Joe, I need to take things
slowly."

"Why?"

"Because I've made some bad decisions in the not too
distant past."

Joe nods, seemingly unimpressed. "And?"

"And I don't want to start a relationship that's only
about sex."

"Me, either," Joe says.

"Oh, please." I laugh, and Joe laughs, too.

"Listen, Mimi. I like you. You like me. How are we going to know where this can go unless we, you know, go with it. What's the point in waiting?"

"I don't want to wait on the relationship. I want to wait on the sex."

Joe says, "Sex is part of an adult relationship."

"But sex confuses the issue. I'm trying to be logical."

"Logical?" Joe leans toward me. "Where's the excitement in that? Where's the passion? A relationship is an organic thing between two people that needs to be nurtured and fed or else it doesn't grow and blossom. Isn't that how you find love?"

More M&M's

"Love and sex are two different things," Madeline says.

Midafternoon, before I have to go to work, Madeline and I are relaxing at the pool in The Garden. Needing analysis of my twenty-four hours with Joe, I called her the minute I got home.

Our towels spread on lounge chairs, Madeline is dousing herself in full-bodied, Italian SPF 30 with citrusy aroma. I opt for a refreshing California SPF 15 that has a hint of wood and olives.

Madeline puts on her cat's eye sunglasses, which are studded with rhinestones. She continues opining. "Joe was either being very romantic, or he wanted to get laid."

"Harsh," I say.

"Realistic," Madeline counters. "You were talking about

sex, and he used the L-word. 'Maybe I'll love you, Mimi, if you boink me.' Please. Do you really think he's in love with you? You hardly know each other. And since when are you a Jersey girl?"

"Since always. No matter where I've gone in the world, I've always been a Jersey girl. Now that I'm back home, I'm rediscovering my inner Jersey girl."

"Speaking of Jersey girls, where's your mother?" Madeline asks.

"Down the shore with her boyfriend," I say. "She left me a note that she's spending a few days in Cape May with Sid. They are staying in a Victorian bed-and-breakfast."

"Now that's romantic."

"Whatever. Can we talk about me and Joe?"

"Sure," Madeline says. "I think you've come down with a serious case of chastity, and I'm not sure it's healthy. Is it because you are living with your mother?"

"My mother is not chaste. She's probably having sex with Sid right now."

"Ugh, gross."

"And so I repress," I say.

"Bobbi's dating bothers you?"

"I know it shouldn't," I say.

"How you feel is how you feel," Madeline replies. "You know what your problem is? Your parents never divorced."

"Having happily married parents is a problem?"

Madeline lowers the straps of her bikini bra. "I went through the whole 'This is Uncle Ted' or 'Meet my new daddy' thing when my parents divorced."

"I don't have a new daddy," I say. "Mom's not going to get remarried. She only just started to date."

Madeline smiles and backstrokes to the subject at hand. "Anyway, Farmer Joe is right that sex is part of an adult relationship. You may want to wait, but he may not want to wait. It sounds like he's got his seduction routine down pat and another Jersey girl might go for it before you decide you're ready."

"You think the whole thing was a seduction routine?"

Madeline turns her cat's eyes to me. "You think he just happened to have a guitar?"

Watermelon vs. Potato

Ah, the serenity of my restaurant mornings. Okay, mid-morning. It's eleven o'clock. Café Louis is clean and the sun pours in through the windows. With XXX coffee in hand, I go into the kitchen. Aaron is standing there, talking with Grammy and Nelson.

"What are you doing here?" I blurt.

"I just came back from the shore," Aaron explains. "I had family stuff all weekend, which is why I couldn't call. So I thought I'd stop by and say hello in person. Hello."

"Hi."

Aaron comes toward me. "How was your weekend?"

"Fine."

"What did you do?" Aaron asks.

"Do? Well, I worked. Of course."

"All weekend?"

"Yes. All weekend."

"Well, that's no good." Aaron puts his hands on my shoulders. "We have to get you some fun. Maybe we can get together one night this week?"

"Yes. Sure. Absolutely."

"Okay. I'll call you." Aaron leans forward and gently kisses me. "Bye."

"Bye."

Aaron turns. "Nice to meet you both."

"You, too," Grammy says, and Nelson nods.

When Aaron leaves the kitchen, Nelson says, "What's that all about? You didn't work all weekend. We were closed half of it."

Instead of answering, I open a newspaper. When I glance up at Grammy, she meets my gaze. Here comes a parable. But no. Grammy simply raises her eyebrows and shakes her head. She doesn't know what's going on, but she disapproves of it all the same. So do I.

On a slow Tuesday night, Fly Girl, Christopher von Hecht, and Bette decide to question me about my love life. I welcome the scrutiny, because I feel badly about seeing both Joe and Aaron. It feels as though I'm cheating on both of them, although I haven't made a commitment to either.

"You went out with both of them," Bette says.

"Right."

"You didn't have sex with Joe or Aaron," Fly Girl says.

"Right."

Bette shrugs. "Then, no. I don't think you are doing anything wrong."

"Good." I put both hands around my coffee mug and lean back in my chair. "Then why does it feel like I'm cheating?"

"If you feel like that, then pick one," Bette says.

"I vote for Aaron," Christopher shouts.

"You don't get a vote, Chrissie. But I should pick Aaron. He's easy to get along with. Joe is sort of prickly. Aaron is clearly interested in a long-term relationship. I think Joe just wants a fling. Joe might be watermelon. Good only in the summer. Aaron is like a potato. Good all year round. But when I'm with Joe, I turn into a big puddle of ish."

Fly Girl pops gum she's not supposed to be chewing. "I think you should keep dating both of them and see what happens. What's the rush to choose? You have time, Mimi."

"Not so much. I want to have kids and I'm not getting any younger."

"But you don't want to rush and make a bad decision," Bette says.

"Right. Because I did that already. Doing it again would be embarrassing."

Allison calls. "I invited Sid and Mom to dinner at my house this weekend. To meet the family."

"Have fun."

"You're coming," Allison says in her mommy voice.

"I already met Sid. And anyway, I have to work."

"Oh, no, Mimi. You can't hide at the restaurant. You are coming. It's a family dinner. You're in the family, right?"

"For now. Did Mom ask you to do this?"

"No," Allison says. "I think it's a nice thing to do. To introduce Sid properly. Make him feel welcome."

I think of how Allison was introduced to our family. Not so properly. Maybe she wants to be the hostess because she sympathizes with Sid's newcomer status. But we knew Allison was staying in the Louis family when we met her. She was seeking permanent residency. Sid's on a temporary visa. Which, I guess, is all the more reason not to overreact.

"And anyway," Allison continues, "you and Jeremy need to stop this childish behavior. Maybe if you get to know Sid, you'll like him."

"Fine, Ally. I'll be there."

Jeez. I didn't know being a good daughter would be so difficult.

◼▬◕ *Promenade*

The afternoon before the family dinner, Aaron asks me to help him buy a birthday present for his sister. He picks me up at the restaurant and we drive to the Promenade, a shopping center that the Scheins didn't build. We browse the ladies of Lily Pulitzer, J. Jill, and Ann Taylor. Finally Aaron buys the newest Coach handbag.

"There's a Sur la Table if you want to look at cookware," Aaron says. We go into the store and I get a contact high from the Le Creuset pots and pans.

"There's a kitchen back there," Aaron says, and we walk to the back of the store.

"I guess they do cooking demonstrations here," I say.

"Look," Aaron says. "Here's the poster announcing the next one."

Smiling from the poster, looking tall and trim in his chef whites, is Nick.

"For the love of Emeril," I mutter.

The ghost of boyfriend past makes me cranky. When Aaron suggests lunch, I say, "I have to go to work."

"But you work at a restaurant," he says. "So that works out well."

Inside Café Louis, I lead Aaron to an empty booth. Christopher instantly materializes. "Lovely to see you, Mr. Schein." He nods at me. "Mrs. Schein."

Aaron laughs, but I don't. "Chrissie? Menus? Please?"

We order—Aaron the chicken salad sandwich and a side of fries, me a bowl of gazpacho—then Aaron says, "What's bothering you?"

To avoid telling him about my ex-boyfriend, I tell Aaron about my mother's current boyfriend. "Tonight my sister-in-law is having a dinner to introduce Sid to the family."

"What do you know about him?" Aaron asks.

"As little as possible," I say.

"Don't you think you should look out for your mother?" Aaron says.

"I am looking out for her," I say.

"A lot of scam artists use the Internet to get money from little old ladies."

"Bobbi Louis is not a little old lady," I say.

"Still," Aaron says. "If my father died and my mom started dating, I'd find out everything I could about her boyfriend. I would feel like it was my responsibility to protect her. Don't you think your father would want you to protect your mother?"

Our food arrives and Aaron eats with his usual gusto. I've lost my appetite.

● ▬◖▭ *Interrogation*

"Sid will be here to pick us up in fifteen minutes." It's the night of the family dinner, and I have made up my mind to find out more about Sid. By asking Mom.

As I finish putting on makeup, I think of all the times Mom and Dad interrogated me about new boyfriends. Who would have thought that the tables would turn?

I know I'm not the only thirty-year-old who has a newly widowed mother diving into the dating pool. I know this because I've read articles about it. Swinging Seniors. Bada Bing Boomers. But what about us kids? How are we to deal with our parents' love lives?

"Mom?" I sit on her bed. "Tell me about Sid."

"What do you want to know?"

Where to start? "He was married?"

"Of course," Mom says. "For thirty years."

"Where is his wife?"

"Beth Israel Cemetery," Mom says.

So Sid is a widower. The death of a spouse. That's something they share. Common ground. Common burial ground. "What did she die of?"

"Cancer," Mom says.

Was it a long death or a short one? I don't need to know that. Moving on. "Does Sid have children?"

"A son." Mom turns to me. "He's single. I could fix you up with him."

"Right. That wouldn't be weird."

Mom laughs.

"What kind of doctor is Sid?"

"A dentist. He retired a few years ago."

There goes the free whitening. "So Sid is financially stable?"

"Yes," Mom says. "I don't know the specifics, but he's certainly comfortable."

"Good."

Mom says, "Any more questions, Detective?"

"I think that's all for now," I say. "You're free to go. But don't leave the country."

Mom laughs. "Actually, we've been talking about leaving the country. To travel. But Sid and his wife traveled around Europe, and he's not keen on going back to places he's already been."

"You've never been to Europe," I say. "Doesn't he want to go with you?"

Mom shrugs. "He's more interested in going to the Caribbean. He wants to relax. Sit in the sun. Play golf."

I can't imagine my mother sitting still for more than a meal. But I don't want to rain on her Caribbean parade, so I refrain from commenting.

"You look pretty, Mimi." Mom runs her hand through my hair, which has grown past my shoulders. The doorbell rings.

◖▭▭▭ *Sidisms*

Mom volunteers to drive to Allison's. "Oh, but I need gas," she says as if this is an insurmountable problem.

Why is Mom acting helpless? As I open my mouth to admonish her, Sid leaps to the rescue. "I'll get you gas."

Mom smiles gratefully. "Thank you, honey."

Sid as he opens the passenger door for her. "Anything for you, Bobbi."

Over Sid's shoulder, Mom winks at me.

She just played him. Played him? No. Mom made Sid feel important. Needed. Valued. She is not helpless. She is certainly capable of getting gas for her car. Why should she if Sid will happily do it for her?

Did Mom do that with Dad? Not that I remember.

Have I ever done that with my boyfriends? Made them feel needed? I don't know. I'm always busy proving how independent I am. Isn't that what Nick told me? I don't need anyone for anything?

Interesting.

Sid drives us to the highway and pulls into the first gas station we see. Mom never, ever pulls into the first gas station. She shops for gas. Not until she's passed at least five gas stations will she select one, even if there is a mere penny's difference in the price. But now she nods and smiles at Sid as he parks in front of the gas pump. She offers her credit card, and Sid says, "My treat."

"Sid is treating? Damn. We should've taken my car," I say somewhat seriously.

"Oh, Mimi." Mom laughs as if I've just said something terribly witty. Sid laughs with Mom, then turns off the car. He gets out of the car and stands near the pump. New Jersey is one of the last states to resist self-serve gas pumps. Attendants abound. There's no need to get out of the car. "What's he doing?" I ask Mom.

"Supervising," Mom answers. "It's an older man thing."

Really? Dad never did that.

Everything in life should be full service, Dad said.

A gas attendant puts the nozzle into the gas tank, and Sid watches the numbers turn as the tank fills. Then he hands the attendant money and the two men nod at each other as if they have concluded a business deal. This strikes me as insane.

Back in the car, Sid says to Mom, "You're all taken care of, sweetheart."

"Thank you, honey."

This is getting a little too sweet for me.

"How about a little music?" Mom suggests as Sid pulls out of the gas station.

"Your mother has a beautiful voice," Sid tells me.

"Thank you, sweetie," Mom says. "Yours is wonderful, too. We make beautiful music together." With that, Mom pushes buttons on her CD player and music comes out of the speakers. Sid clears his throat and Mom waves her hands to the music. And then . . .

They sing. They harmonize.

I know this car has air bags. Does it have barf bags?

📠 *Meet the Children*

Sarah is waiting for us on the brick steps of her home. She looks up at Sid. "What am I supposed to call you?" she asks. "I have a Grandpa and a Zadie."

"Do you have a Sid?" he asks.

Although she accepts Sid's initial effort, Sarah remains aloof toward him. I watch Sarah watch Sid, and part of me—the really immature part of me—is grateful that she's on my side. The rest of the Louis family is being exceedingly polite to Sid. Even Jeremy. He must have gotten a talking-to from his wife.

As for Allison, she is in rare form. I volunteer to help her finish dinner.

"I can do it," she insists.

"I know you can do it, Ally. But let me help. I'll be your sous chef."

"My what?" She looks at me with crazed eyes.

"Your assistant. Tell me what to do. You're the boss."

"Fine. Good. Thanks. Can you handle the macaroni and cheese? And the mashed potatoes?"

"That's what we're having for dinner?" I ask. "Not that I'm judging."

Allison tosses her salad and explains. "The twins want chicken fingers and mashed potatoes. It's easier to give them what they want then have them throw a fit in front of company. But Sarah has decided that she's not eating brown food. So, I'm making her a hot dog and the macaroni and cheese. The grown-up food is brisket, rice pilaf, creamed spinach, and corn soufflé. Oh, crap. I forgot about the soufflé."

Allison dives into the oven and removes the soufflé. From where I'm standing, I can see that the soufflé is burnt. Allison watches the soufflé cave in on itself. "Oh, no," Allison says. "Now what am I going to do?"

"Here, gimme." I take the casserole dish from her. With a serving spoon, I take off the burnt crust and scoop the rest of the soufflé into another bowl. "See? All better."

"Thanks, Mimi."

"Why the crazy?" I ask, hoping there's no earth-shattering reason. "You want to tell me what's bothering you?"

Allison exhales. "Next week, my mother is coming to visit."

Phoebe Greene travels from Boca Raton to Jersey twice a year, during Chanukah and August. Since her husband died seven years ago, Phoebe has traveled quite a lot more than she did when Hal Greene's work schedule kept them in Florida. Hal was a real estate developer who left his widow a comfortable fortune, which Phoebe spends freely. Almost as freely as she dispenses advice on how Allison should cook, eat, dress, and parent.

I adore Phoebe. But I have the advantage of not being her daughter.

"You have all week to worry about your mother," I tell Allison. "Tonight, let's worry about mine."

Other than the corn soufflé, dinner goes perfectly. The twins tell Sid about their preschool teachers, and he tells them about his grandsons. "You would like them," Mom tells the boys. "They are the same age as you and very nice."

Mom's met Sid's family? That's news. Jeremy looks at me with raised eyebrows. I see his eyebrows and raise him a shrug.

As Mom, Sid, and I say our goodbyes, Sarah gives me a big hug, then looks at me with her big brown eyes. Quietly she says, "Are you thinking about Zadie?"

I blink a few times, then say, "Yes."

Sarah nods. "Me, too," she says.

On the drive back to The Garden, Mom tells me that she is—shock of shocks—spending the night at Sid's. That's when I remember that I forgot to talk to Mom about spending time with Allison. It's not right to tell her now, in front of Sid. Plus Allison will be busy with her own mother.

My mother walks me to the front door of the condo. "Mimi? Thanks."

"For what?"

Mom smiles. "Making Sid feel welcome."

"You're welcome."

▬▬◖ Collingswood

Farmer Joe calls to ask me for a date. With him working days at the farm and me working nights at Café Louis, the only time we can find is Saturday morning-ish. Joe says that he will be manning a booth at a street fair in Collingswood, and I agree to meet him there. Collingswood is between Cherry Hill and Philadelphia. It's a ten-minute drive from either place. I drive Sally to Haddon Avenue, the town's main drag. I have never been to Collingswood, and I'm surprised at the quaint calm of the town.

White tents canopy the street, their peaks looking like egg whites progressing down Haddon Avenue as far as I can see. Lampposts are decorated with flowers; baskets of purple and gold impatiens hang around the lampposts' midsections, just below royal blue banners that read "Welcome to Historic Collingswood" in white letters. "Established 1883." Red brick buildings line the street, giving Haddon Avenue the feel of a real American Main Street. Not that I would know what that looks like. I am a child of the mall generation. But I'd like to think that life was once like this, with independent, family-owned shops doing a brisk business among neighbors. It's very Huck Finnish. I like it.

"Collingswood T-shirts," calls a young man standing in front of a display.

Crafty art is for sale under the tents, as are decorative masks, beaded jewelry, dried flower arrangements, ceramic and glass garden ornaments, and handpainted T-shirts.

"Collingswood T-shirts. Atkins friendly," the man calls.

Warm dough smell drifts from Joe's Pizza Parlor. Farther down the street, a big man stirs a pot of Kettle Corn while his colleague passes out sample handfuls. Crepes are cooked under a hot griddle, and the sizzle reaches my ears. Area bakeries do a brisk business selling cookies, individually sized pies and breads. Flower merchants wrap purple lilies and pink tulips in yellow paper. Folksy rock comes from a live band on the tented grandstand.

"Collingswood T-shirts. Perfect gift for Christmas, birthdays, and Bar Mitzvahs."

Friends greet each other warmly with hugs and handshakes. Even the teenagers have left their melancholy at home. In front of the jewelry tents, men in khaki shorts and golfing shirts wait for wives wearing cotton capri pants and scoop-necked shirts. White-haired men and women shuffle slowly along the sidewalk. A stroller brigade winds its way through the crowd.

In the middle of Haddon Avenue, I spot Joe under a sign with the state slogan: "Jersey Fresh." Got that right. Joe greets me with a tongue kiss that tastes peppery, like arugula. Sure enough, I spot a bag of baby lettuce under the table. "Tico, you okay here for a while?" Joe asks the man wearing a Hunter Farm T-shirt.

Joe and I walk hand in hand down Haddon Avenue. "This is a nice town," I say.

"I come here a lot," Joe says. He points to a sign that says "Dr. Cohen." "There's my dentist's office," he says. I wave.

Joe nods and steers me down a street, away from the noise of the fair. We walk a few blocks and come to Cooper River. "Pull up a bench," Joe says, and sits on one overlooking the river. "What's new?"

"Well, we had a family dinner for my mom's boyfriend."

"Your mom is dating?" Joe seems shocked.

I give the details, then ask, "How would you feel if your mother was dating?"

Joe laughs. "My mother is in no condition to date. Sometimes she thinks my father is still alive."

"Her memory is going?"

"The doctors say it's early onset Alzheimer's. She's only sixty-three." Joe looks out at the river. "It's too soon."

"You take good care of your mom," I say.

"I try," Joe says. "There are a lot of people around during the day. Everyone who works on the farm checks in on her. At some point, I'll have to find a facility for her. I keep putting it off. I'm not ready to let her go."

I put my hand in Joe's. He squeezes.

"You're lucky that your mom is healthy," Joe says.

"Yeah, I am."

Joe says, "I think it's the slowness of the deterioration that bothers me most. I want to die like my father died. He keeled over in the fields. That's what he would've wanted. No hospitals. Just—boom. Done. Nature taking its course." Joe puts his hand over mine. "What about your father?"

"There was nothing natural about his death," I say. "He was hooked up to tubes and machines. The doctors were feeding him intravenously, and you know what Dad said? 'Needs a little salt.' "

Joe laughs. He puts his arm around me. I move closer to his body. Looking at Cooper River, Joe says, "I'm sorry that I didn't get to meet your dad."

Tears spring into my eyes. What is this with Joe? He

says these sentimental things that make me all emotional. Blinking, I say, "You'd have liked my dad. And I'm sorry I didn't get to meet your father."

"Oh, he would have loved you." Joe leans his head against mine.

We sit quietly.

Eventually, I speak. "Fun date, huh?"

"It's not so bad. I like talking about my dad."

"Me, too. It's good to have you to talk to, Joe."

"Yeah? Well, I think we've had enough talking." Joe moves my head backward and puts his mouth on mine. We sit in the sun, kissing.

⬤▭🍴 *Mango Men*

"Joe is such a good kisser." Madeline has come to Café Louis for dinner, and I'm updating her on the Joe-Aaron situation. "Aaron's good, too."

Madeline is eating French fries for dinner. Even chefs eat junk food. Madeline points a fry at me. "Did you give them the mango test?"

"What's the mango test?" Christopher asks as he sashays down the counter.

"Is this a sex thing?" Fly Girl appears from nowhere. "Tell me."

Madeline smiles. "If a man will eat a mango, he'll eat you."

"I'm going to vomit," Christopher says.

Fly Girl frowns. "I thought that test was about sushi."

I say, "That equates women with raw fish. That's not right."

"Plus, sushi comes with rice," Madeline explains. "And soy sauce. Or a man could say that he eats sushi, but all he really eats is a California roll. Which doesn't even have raw fish. Nope, mangoes are the way to go. Mimi and I have given this much thought."

"You guys rock," Fly Girl says.

"How old are you?" It suddenly occurs to me that this may not be age-appropriate for her.

"I'm twenty," she tells me.

"The other thing," Madeline continues, "is that it's not simply if he will eat a mango, but how. Does he use a knife and cut the mango into small pieces?"

I say, "Does he cut the mango into big, juicy slices?"

"Or . . ." Madeline laughs. "Does he bite into the mango and get the juice all over his face?"

"Gross beyond gross," Christopher moans.

"Then stop listening, Chrissie," I tell him. "Anyway, no. I haven't given either Joe or Aaron the mango test. But I'm sure Joe eats mangoes, and eats them well. He knows food."

"I bet chefs make great lovers," Fly Girl says dreamily.

"We do." Madeline grins.

"Even the men?" Fly Girl asks.

"Male chefs make great lovers but bad boyfriends," Madeline tells her. "On the plus side, they are used to putting all kinds of things in their mouths. They are very sensual. They pay attention to details. Also, they have lots of time in the afternoon between lunch and dinner. Chef sex in the afternoon. Nothing like it. So, by all means, have sex with a chef. Just don't date one."

"Don't tell her that," I reprimand. "She's young and im-pressionable."

"Better she learn now," Madeline answers as she chews on a French fry.

"If chefs are great lovers, why not date them?" Fly Girl asks.

"Because," Madeline continues, "he'll work nights, weekends, and holidays. He'll be dictatorial, because in the kitchen he's the big boss and he won't turn it off at home. Also? Think of all the waitresses running around as temptations."

I groan.

"Sorry," Madeline apologizes.

"It's all right," I tell her. "Seems like ages ago. I'm ready for a new mango man."

Christopher leans over the counter. "Do you think the same test works with bananas?"

Here Comes the Sun

Humidity is my least favorite thing about summer. It builds, rises, increases until it's hard to breathe and im-possible not to sweat. If humidity had a color, it would be gray. London gray. Los Angeles gray. Like smog. But we don't have smog in Jersey. Not yet, anyway. The only good thing about humidity is that it leads to summer storms, which are a sight to behold.

God's letting off a little steam, Dad said. He can only take so much. Look what happened to Noah.

As I stand outside Café Louis on the first day of August, I see the color drain from the sky. Clouds don't really gather for a summer storm. They disperse, actually, running hard and fast from God's temper tantrum. In their haste to get away, the clouds shed, leaving a blanket of gray in their wake. It makes the sky look like a ceiling.

Next comes the breeze. It's cool and crisp and smells green from all the trees it has swept through on its way here. The breeze is refreshing, and even though I know it's a trick, that the breeze is lulling me into a false sense of security, I close my eyes and let it blow through my hair.

Thunder, soft at first. It sounds like the rumbling of a highway under a Mack truck. It's another warning.

Look out below, Dad said.

The thunder builds, like the rising drumbeat of an orchestra. Then comes the lightning in quick shots, adding the crash of a cymbal to the overture.

The first drops hit my face gently, and I know I should go inside the restaurant. One, two, three drops. Boom. Crash. Four, five, six drops. Boom. Crash.

Then the heavens open and dump water in bucketfuls. Stepping under the awning of the restaurant, I listen to the steady rhythm of the rain bouncing against the concrete steps and the asphalt of the parking lot. It sounds like applause.

Five minutes pass, and I watch, hypnotized. The skies begin to clear before the rain stops. The gray ceiling fades and the sky lightens to a pastel blue. The rain's intensity abates, quickly slowing to a drizzle. The applause fades. The show is over.

Here comes the sun.

▰▱◣ *Phoebe Greene*

She's here.

To celebrate Phoebe's arrival, I have been summoned to Allison's house in the middle of the day. Because I'm working the dinner shift at Café Louis, I can't stay for long. If I could, I would glue myself to Phoebe for the duration of her visit. The woman knows how to live, love, and look fabulous.

Allison's house smells gold, the color of simmering chicken soup. Chicken soup in the summer? Why is Allison doing this to herself?

Walking into the kitchen, I see Phoebe and Allison huddled over the stove, their backs to me. Allison is wearing a black tank top and white skirt with black heels. From behind, I can tell that Allison has styled her hair into fat curls, which her mother prefers. But the humidity and cooking steam have undone most of Allison's curls and her head is now a mishmash of straight strands and loosening waves.

As for Phoebe, she is a riot of color next to black and white–clad Allison. Phoebe wears a silk top festooned with triangles of jewel-toned blue, green, orange, and red. Her black pants are fitted to her trim waist and hips.

Phoebe's dyed blond hair is teased high, making its drop to her shoulders more dramatic.

"I'm trying to show you the right way to make chicken soup," Phoebe tells Allison.

Doesn't Allison know how to make chicken soup? Yes, I'm quite sure she does. Allison's hair isn't the only thing approaching a meltdown. She hands her mother a wooden spoon and turns her back on the stove. "Look, Mom. Mimi's here."

Phoebe turns to smile at me. Eyes. She had her eyes done.

For the past few years, Phoebe has arrived in Jersey with part of her body newly restructured. She started with a tummy tuck. Breast lift, thigh lipo, arm lipo, butt lift, lower back lipo, chin lipo, laser removal of age spots. Because she has the work done gradually, Phoebe doesn't look drastically different from visit to visit. But there's always something. Now it's her eyes. It doesn't look like a drastic brow lift. Perhaps it was something on the eyelids. I'll ask her later. Phoebe is honest about her cosmetic procedures. She considers them to be part of her job as a woman. Maintenance, she calls it.

"Mimi!" Phoebe abandons the stove, leaving Allison free to dump a handful of herbs into the disputed pot. Enrobing me in a light, musky scent, Phoebe gives me a strong hug.

"How are you?" I ask. She waves away my question.

"What is this about your boyfriend cheating on you?"

"Mom!" But there's no point in Allison trying to deflect or protect me from her mother's questions. When it comes to men, Phoebe Greene is the self-appointed expert. Of course, Allison could've avoided the whole thing by not telling her mother about Nick's transgressions. As if reading my mind, Phoebe says, "I asked Jeremy about your love life. So, what? He cheated on you and you left?"

Mom walks into the kitchen holding sippy cups. She says, "Oh, Mimi, you're finally here." I look at my watch and see that I am right on time. Mom goes to the refrigerator to refill sippy cups. "What are you girls talking about?"

"Mimi is telling me the story of her boyfriend cheating on her," Phoebe says.

Without looking up from the jar of apple juice, Mom raises her eyebrows. But she doesn't interrupt. So Phoebe continues. "Tell me."

I shrug. "There's nothing else to say."

"You caught him?"

I nod.

"Doing what?"

Mom isn't looking at me, and Allison's back is to us. No help.

"This girl was giving him . . . oral . . ." I say.

"A blow job?" Phoebe asks.

"Well. Yeah."

Phoebe waves her fingers at Allison. "What do I always say about blow jobs? You see? I was right."

Allison groans.

Phoebe smacks her hands together, making her gold and silver bangles crash around her wrists. She turns to me. "That's what men want."

"Blow jobs?" I reply.

"Sex," she answers. "Men want sex, money, and food. They want the money to buy food. They want the food to have strength to have sex. It's simple."

"Okay." I can't argue with her logic. I can't argue with her at all.

"Also, don't cut your hair short," Phoebe commands. "Never. You want to keep your man? No short hair. They like it long." She points to her daughter. "Like Allison's hair. Beautiful. She wanted to cut it short when her twins were born. I told her no. Right, Allison?"

"Yes, Mom."

"You see?" Phoebe says proudly. "I was right."

Finished refilling the sippy cups, Mom heads out of the kitchen. As she passes Allison, Mom rubs her back and gives her a quick kiss on the cheek. Mom leaves me standing under Phoebe's sex spotlight.

"Another thing," she continues. "Don't stop shaving and waxing. Men don't want to see hair growing on their women. You're sick? You're pregnant? It doesn't matter. You get out of bed and get a razor. You need help? Get your mother to help. We've done worse."

Sarah walks quietly into the room. "Aunt Mimi," she says with a smile, "come play with us." Sarah puts her hand in mine and pulls me away. Thank the goddess.

◼▬◖ *Latin Lover*

Hot tamale. That's what I think when I lay my eyes on the hunk of burning Banderas standing in Allison's living room. Dark skin, black eyes, black hair that is wavy in all the right places. Wide shoulders, wide lips, and a sexy smile. Which is directed at me. Is he an early birthday gift from Phoebe? It would be just like her to bring me a stud. "You need a Latin lover," she'll probably tell me.

Ezra and Gideon are pulling at my hands. I shake them lose and walk toward the handsome man. I smile. And then Jeremy is standing in front of me. "Mimi," he says. "I have to talk to you."

"Can't I meet the gorgeous man first?"

Jeremy laughs and whispers in my ear. "That's Phoebe's boyfriend."

I gasp. "No!"

"Oh, yes," Jeremy says. "When we went to the airport to get Phoebe, there he was."

"You and Ally didn't know he was coming?"

Jeremy shakes his head. "We didn't know he existed."

"Oy."

"Double oy," Jeremy says.

"Are they staying in a hotel?"

"Nope," Jeremy says. "They are in our house. In the same bedroom."

"He looks Latino," I whisper, eyeballing the man over Jeremy's shoulder.

Jeremy nods. "She met him in Buenos Aires."

"What was Phoebe doing in Buenos Aires?" I want to know.

"I have no idea. What is she ever doing anywhere?"

"How old is this guy?" I ask Jeremy.

He shrugs, and peers into the living room. "Late thirties? Early forties?"

"At least our mom dates men her own age."

Jeremy smiles. "I guess Phoebe likes younger men."

"And they like her."

This Latin lover, whose name is Enrique, is so completely under Phoebe's spell that it's difficult not to laugh at him. When Phoebe walks into a room, Enrique's face brightens. When she is near him, Phoebe touches Enrique in a feminine way that makes him look more masculine. Gently, she leans on him. She turns her head to look up at him, although they are almost the same height because she is wearing stilettos.

They aren't doing anything, really. They don't have their arms around each other. They aren't holding hands. But I feel like a peeping Tom, even though there's nothing to see. Like Enrique, I can't take my eyes off Phoebe. When she leaves his side, Enrique watches her walk, unabashedly rolling his eyes over her body. Her sixty-something-year-old body. Maybe Phoebe's right about something. Or everything.

━━◗☜ *Mothers*

Out of the corner of my eye, I see Allison standing in the kitchen watching her mother. She looks very sad. No one sees her but me, so I slowly make my way to her. When she sees me coming, Allison turns and disappears into the kitchen. I follow her.

"Are you okay?" I ask.

Allison nods, then shakes her head. "She's acting like a fool. What is she thinking? That man is twenty years younger than she is."

"But he makes her happy. You said that about Mom and Sid. Remember?"

Allison frowns. "I understand now. What makes you upset about Sid. It's not who he is. It's who he isn't. Your father."

"Yeah," I say. "I guess that's what it is."

Allison puts her hand on my shoulder. "I'm sorry I didn't understand."

"It's okay. Let's blame our mothers."

"Sounds good to me," Allison says with a smile.

━━◗☜ *I Believe in Love*

Aaron Schein is waiting for me at Café Louis. As the servers set up the restaurant for dinner, Aaron talks with Bette at the counter. I smile at them. "That's a dreamy look," Bette says.

Sitting on a stool, I say, "I just met a very handsome man."

"Who?" Bette and Aaron say.

"Enrique," I say. "He's tall and dark and mysterious."

"Go on," Bette says.

"He was just so . . . passionate. Like he believes in love."

"And?" Aaron is unimpressed.

"You wouldn't understand."

"What wouldn't I understand?" Aaron says.

"Passion."

"I understand passion," Aaron insists. "I'm all about passion."

Bette raises her eyebrows and drifts to the other end of the counter. I smile at Aaron, but the passion between Phoebe and Enrique has me thinking about Farmer Joe and his passion for farming, the ocean, his guitar, and me. "What are you passionate about, Aaron? What do you believe in?"

"Lots of things."

"Tell me."

Aaron thinks for a few minutes, then stands. "I believe in supply-side economics. I believe that Kurt Cobain was a genius. I believe that California wines are just as good as European wines. I believe in two-point conversions. I believe there is intelligent life on other planets. I believe Al Gore won the 2000 election. I believe in stem cell research, but not cloning. I believe William Shakespeare wrote alone. I believe in love. I believe in *b'shaert*, the fateful meeting of two people who are meant to be together forever. I believe that when you find your soul mate, you love her and cherish her for the rest of your life."

Aaron finishes his speech, and breathes. "How's that?"

"Pretty good." Seriously.

"Good," Aaron says. "Listen, Christopher says the restaurant will probably have a slow weekend. My sister's birthday party is this weekend at my family's house in Avalon. Why don't you come? What's a Jersey girl without weekends down the shore? You haven't had a break all summer."

That's not exactly true, is it? I had my Fourth of July fireworks with Farmer Joe on LBI. But Aaron doesn't need to know about that.

I say, "I'd love to come to Avalon."

The next morning, I'm surprised to see Mom sitting at the kitchen table. "You look like a woman who used to live here," I tell her.

Mom doesn't answer. Her lips are pressed together, and she's staring at a felt-covered jewelry box. I walk around Mom's chair and look over her shoulder. She's staring at a diamond ring. It looks like the engagement ring Dad gave her. Mom stopped wearing it when Dad bought her a channel-set diamond band for their twenty-fifth anniversary. Why is Mom staring at her engagement ring? She must be thinking about Dad.

I put my hand on Mom's shoulder. "Is that the ring Daddy gave you?"

"No," Mom says. "It's the ring Sid gave me."

■━◗ *The Ring Thing*

"Want to see it?" Mom offers me the velvet box.

"No." I back away from the box as if it is evil.

"It's a gorgeous ring." Mom gazes at the ring. "You are very pretty. Yes, you are."

"Sid asked you to marry him."

"Yes." Mom looks at me with a small smile and big eyes. She wants to know what I think. Please, I silently beg, don't ask me what I think.

"I know what you think," Mom says. "You don't want me to marry Sid."

"You haven't known him that long. Isn't it too soon? That's what you said about me and Nick. What happened to taking things slowly?"

Mom nods and purses her lips. "I didn't say yes."

"Oh. What did you say?"

"That I care for him very much but I need some time to think."

"Good. That's good." I lean against the kitchen counter. "What do you think?"

"I love you very much, Mimi, but I don't want to share that with you."

I blink a few times. "Okay."

"I'm still your mother. I hope you'll respect whatever decision I make."

*   *   *

Why do I feel this way? Driving to the restaurant, I tell myself to be happy for Mom. But it comes down to this. I can't be happy about Mom without being sad about Dad.

⊫⊏ *Grammy Love, Part Two*

"Good morning," Grammy greets me. "Nellie's at the doctor's. He'll be here before lunch starts."

"Okay."

Grammy looks at my face. "What's the matter?"

I look at the concern in Grammy's face, and feel that I can tell her anything. "Mom's boyfriend proposed to her."

"Well, now." Grammy looks down at the bowl in front of her. "What do you think about that?"

"I'm trying to think happy thoughts. But they aren't coming."

Grammy works quietly. I drink my coffee and look out the back door of the restaurant. With her back to me, Grammy says, "Your mother loving this new man doesn't mean she didn't love your father."

"But Sid is so different from Dad."

"Good thing," Grammy says.

"What does that mean?"

Grammy sighs. "Bobbi didn't have it easy with Jay. He worked all the time. Long restaurant hours. Weekend nights. Holidays."

"Dad made it up to us." I turn back to the worktable.

"To you," Grammy says. "Maybe not to her."

"Is that why Mom wanted me to sell the restaurant? Because she resents it?"

"I can't speak for your mother," Grammy says.

▬▬◖ *More M&M's*

Madeline comes when I call her. She sits in a booth at Café Louis, facing me as I tell her my tale of maternal marriage. When I finish, Madeline narrows her eyes. "And?"

"What do you mean 'and'?"

"And Bobbi gets married to Sid. What's the big?"

I stare at Madeline. How can she not understand how this makes me feel? While I try to find the words to explain it, Madeline takes a sip of her root beer and adjusts the slipping strap of her white tank top. Finally she says, "This whole getting to know your family as an adult? It's rough. It's like, where do you fit into the family? Your brother has his own family. Your mom has her own thing. And you don't know where that leaves you. Am I right?"

"Yes. You're exactly right."

Madeline nods and plays with her straw. "Growing up sucks."

I agree. "Everything was so much easier when we were young. Younger. Like even five years ago. When I was twenty-five, I had my whole life ahead of me. Now I know what I want but I can't get it."

"You still think you want . . ."

"Husband. Children. Career. Everything."

"So, Mimi, how exactly would you do that? Assuming you save Café Louis, how would you manage a family and the restaurant?"

"My dad did it."

"Your dad had your mom," Madeline says. "If you're going to be like your dad, maybe you need to marry someone like your mom."

"Meaning?"

"Someone supportive. Your mom supported your dad for years."

"Yeah," I agree. "She did."

Madeline smiles. "Your mom's pretty amazing."

"Yes. She is."

What's for Dinner?

Driving to the townhouse, I tell myself that Mom should marry Sid. Why shouldn't she? Mom deserves every happiness she can find.

"Mom? Mom?" I rush into the townhouse and find Mom in her bathroom, wearing her nightgown and removing her makeup.

"What?" she says. "What's the matter?"

I stand before Mom, towering over her. "You should marry Sid."

Mom puts her palm on my forehead. "Are you sick? Do you have a temperature?"

"No, I'm not sick." I move away from her hand. "I want you to be happy."

"I am happy," Mom says. "I don't need to marry Sid to be happy."

"So you're not going to marry him?"

"I don't know yet." Mom smears cream on her face. "We've only been dating for three months. I thought about what you said. It's too soon. You were right."

"No, no. I was wrong. It's statistically impossible for me to be right."

"And there's something else. Something happened."

Do I want to know? "What happened?"

"The other day, we were sitting on Sid's deck reading magazines. Oh, forget it."

"Okay."

"No, I'll tell you. It's silly, but . . ." Mom looks at me with white goop all over her face. She wants to tell me.

"Mom. What is it?"

"We were sitting there, and we'd been lounging around all day. At about five o'clock, Sid turns to me and says, 'What's for dinner?' "

" 'What's for dinner?' "

"Yeah." Mom puts her hands on her hips. "Can you believe that?"

I don't get Mom's indignation. Part of me wants to jump on any excuse to berate Sid. But the other part of me . . . "I don't understand. What's wrong with asking about dinner?"

Mom throws her hands in the air. "Why should he assume that I'm the one who will cook dinner?"

"You don't usually cook dinner?"

"No," Mom says. "We cook together. Or we go out. That

was the first time Sid assumed that dinner was my responsibility."

"Maybe he was simply asking what you wanted to eat for dinner. Like, 'What are we going to do about dinner?' "

"There was no 'we,' " Mom says. "So, I got up from my very comfortable seat on the deck. And I made dinner. But you know what, Mimi? I don't want to make dinner every night for someone. I did that for years. For you and Jeremy and your dad. I don't want to do it again."

I see what Mom is saying. Could this be what breaks up her and Sid? Do I want it to be? Sort of. However . . .

"Mom, did you talk to Sid about this?"

"No." She turns her back to me and fusses with her face cream.

I lean against the bathroom door. "Well, maybe you should . . ."

"And another thing." Mom turns around again. "I haven't been to a library lecture or a synagogue luncheon for weeks. Maybe months. What about my breakfast club with Ally? I haven't done that, either. Nor have I spent time with Sarah and the twins."

"Or me."

"Right! Look at you, Mimi. You need me. You're still a mess."

"Hey!"

"Sorry," Mom says. "But I haven't spent nearly enough time with you."

So, she knows. Mom knows that her time with Sid has been taking her away from her family and her other activities. But is that Sid's fault or Mom's responsibility? It sounds like Mom is talking through fear, making excuses for not marrying Sid. Am I supposed to point this out to her?

I so don't want to be in this position. And yet . . .

"Mom, maybe you could balance things a little better. Have you thought about that? Giving that a try?"

Mom smiles at me. "Are you giving me relationship advice?"

"Don't think it's not painful for me."

Mom turns back to her mirror. "I'll let you know when I make my decision. In the meantime, don't mention Sid's proposal to Ally or Jeremy. They have enough to worry about with Phoebe and her lover."

"Okay." I exhale. This conversation has exhausted me. "I'm going to bed."

"Don't forget that we have a girls' lunch tomorrow."

"Girls?"

"Me, Phoebe, Ally, and you. At Ally's house. Noon."

"I'll be there."

❧ Girls of All Ages

"What does his family do?" Phoebe asks me.

"Real estate." I'm being held for questioning in the matter of my love life. Explaining Aaron is easier than explaining Joe. Phoebe, Mom, and I are sitting on Allison's sunny deck, waiting for dessert. Allison is busy making herself crazy in the kitchen. Lunch was a delicious summer salad with grilled chicken, although I'm the thing getting grilled.

"Ah, real estate," Phoebe says approvingly. This is the field in which her husband made his fortune. "His family has money?"

"Yes," I say.

"Excellent." Phoebe approves.

"Money isn't the most important thing," Mom says. "I want Mimi to be with someone she loves."

"She can't love this one?" Phoebe asks.

Mom is saved from retorting by Allison's emergence onto the deck. She's carrying a fruit salad made with honeydew, mango, kiwi, and strawberries. Phoebe smiles approvingly. "Very pretty, sweetheart."

"Thanks, Mom." Allison smiles. She scoops fruit into glass dishes.

Phoebe keeps talking. "My daughter did the right thing. Married a nice man with a good job who supports her while she raises their children."

There are so many errors in that statement that I am shocked she actually made it. Does she not know that Allison married Jeremy because she was pregnant? Maybe she doesn't know. Maybe it doesn't matter.

"Mimi, you should have children while you are young," Phoebe states. "That way, you can enjoy your life when you get older. Like me and Bobbi. We have our freedom."

Mom smiles politely.

"I'm trying, Phoebe," I tell her. "I'm trying to find the perfect husband so I can become the perfect mother and wife. Just like Ally."

"Actually, I'm thinking about getting a job." Ally says this quietly, looking at her bowl of fruit. "The twins will be in kindergarten in September. I'd like to work. I think I should get a job."

Phoebe waves her spoon in the air. "Don't be ridiculous, sweetheart. You have a job. Two jobs. Mother and wife."

"I would have time to do something else."

"So you can be tired and unhappy all the time?" Phoebe laughs. "You think you have time to work, but you don't. Just because the boys aren't home all day doesn't mean you stop cooking and cleaning for them. You know what will happen, sweetheart? You will do things you don't need to do and stop doing things you must do."

"Like blow jobs," I offer.

"Exactly," Phoebe says.

Sisters-in-Law, Part Four

Allison clears dishes and looks like she's going to implode. I follow her into the kitchen. "Phoebe's pretty tough on you, huh?"

"It's not her. It's you."

"Me? What'd I do?"

Allison deposits dishes into the sink, then turns to me. "I'm tired of you saying that I'm perfect. That I have a perfect life."

"But you do. You have everything. I want what you have."

Allison laughs. "You want what I have? I want what you have."

"What do I have? I don't have anything."

"Exactly." Allison points her finger at me. "You don't have anything. No responsibilities. Me? I'm responsible to everyone for everything. My husband, my children, my mother, your mother. You? You take care of yourself. I take care of everyone but myself."

Egad. I don't know what to say, so I don't say anything.

Allison folds her arms over her chest and leans backward against the kitchen counter. She breathes deeply. "Don't misunderstand, Mimi. I know that I'm lucky to have a great house, a great family, and a great husband. It's just . . ."

"Go ahead," I tell her. "Say it."

"All summer, you've been saying that you want to get married and have kids and you've been holding me up as a role model. But really, Mimi, I don't think you have the slightest idea what it means to be a wife and mother. It's difficult. And it's forever."

"Are you sorry?" I ask quietly. "Are you sorry that you are a wife and mother?"

"No. But some days, I wonder what else I could've been."

Wow. I lean against the kitchen island, opposite my sister-in-law, and absorb what she's said. A soft breeze blows through the open windows, ruffling the curtains.

Allison exhales. "Sorry. I shouldn't have said all that."

"I'm glad you did."

"Well, I do feel better." Allison laughs. "So, thanks. For listening."

I smile at her. "Ally, I know what your mother said, but there's no reason you can't get a job. If you want one."

"I need a job," she answers. "We need money."

"Really?"

"Yes, Mimi. Don't look so shocked. We need money for the mortgage, two car payments, Sarah's piano lessons and her dance class. The twins need clothes and supplies for kindergarten in September, which means we can't afford a summer vacation this year. Why do you think I've been asking about the finances at the restaurant?"

"Oh. I didn't realize." Exactly how self-absorbed have I been? A lot, it seems.

"We'll figure it out." Allison waves her hands in the air. "It's not your problem."

"I'm part of this family," I state. "It is my problem. But, look. The restaurant is turning a profit. A small one, but it's something. I was thinking about reinvesting it in new kitchen equipment. But you can have it. It's only a few thousand dollars, but it will help."

"Really?" Allison looks grateful. So grateful that I feel guilty for not offering to help long before this.

"Of course," I tell her. "The money is yours."

⬤━◖ Greetings from Asbury Park

Back at Café Louis, I think about everything Allison said. Then I remember what Allison said about vacation. I call Mom and find her at home.

"Mom, remember when Jeremy and I were kids and Dad closed the restaurant for the last week of August so we could have a family vacation at the shore? Why don't we do that again? We could rent a four-bedroom house, or a three-bedroom with a sleeper sofa."

"That'd be nice, Mimi."

"Great. How do you feel about splitting the cost with me? Jeremy and Ally have a lot of financial commitments. But Ally definitely needs a vacation before school starts and the kids' schedules get hectic. Anyway, I think they'd be more inclined to come down the shore if they didn't have to pay to rent a house. Can you and I split the cost?"

"You would do that?" Mom sounds surprised.

"I would," I tell her. "I have money saved from my Dine International days."

"Well, Mimi, you don't have to pay for it. I'll be happy to. We should absolutely have a family vacation. I don't know why I didn't think of it myself. Listen, I'll make some phone calls. It's late in the season, but I'll try Sea Isle, Wildwood, Cape May, and Long Beach Island. All of the houses may be rented."

"Why don't we try a northern shore town?"

"Like where?" Mom asks.

I root around in the desk for the postcard that says "To J, All my love, B." Where was that card from? Asbury Park.

"Mom, how about Asbury Park? What's it like?"

"I don't know," Mom says. "I've never been to Asbury Park."

▄▅◁ *Lipstick Theory Three*

She's wrong. Mom is wrong. She's remembering wrong. How could she remember a vacation she took ten years ago?

I stare at the postcard. I look at the kiss. Then I look at the lipstick. It's pink. Mom's been wearing mulberry lipstick for decades. I've never seen her wear pink lipstick.

"How does that sound, Mimi?"

"Fine, Mom." I haven't heard a word she's said.

"Okay. I'll make some more calls and let you know what I discover."

What have I discovered?

"To J, All my love, B."

The J could stand for Jeremy. From the postmark, I see the card was sent ten years ago. Jeremy was getting his MBA at Wharton. He was single. Maybe some girl sent him a postcard. Why would she send it to the restaurant? Did Jeremy work here the summer before he met Allison? No. I did. Jeremy was doing an internship in Manhattan. The J has to be Jay. Dad.

Who is B? Who is the pink lipstick–wearing B?

Bette.

Ordering slips. I have Bette's handwritten ordering slips. I can compare the handwriting on the slips to the handwriting on the postcard. Scrambling through the piles on the desk, I find Bette's slips.

But then I stop. I put the ordering slips back on the desk. I turn the postcard to its picture side, hiding the handwriting. I close my eyes.

◼━━◖ *Mustard Memories, Part Two*

My mind drifts to my childhood, and those nights when Dad came home late and made sandwiches with good mustard. Why did Dad get home at midnight if the restaurant closed at nine during the week? Why was Dad hungry if he had just left the restaurant? Why didn't Dad come on vacations with me, Mom, and Jeremy? What did he do while we were away? What does Mom know? Is that why she wants me and Jeremy to sell Café Louis, be rid of it once and for all? Is that why she didn't want me to work here? Because I might uncover the secret she's kept for so long?

I know chefs, do I?

No. That can't be right. Dad loved Mom. He wasn't a cheater. Dad wasn't a Nick.

But what if Dad had an affair with Bette? What does that mean? To Mom? To me?

Here I sit, with a choice before me. I could CSI my family and find the truth about Dad. I could compare handwriting samples, search for more clues, interrogate Bette, and build a case against my father. But the dead body in the middle of the case would still be dead, and part of me might die, too. I might have to spend years in therapy discussing my father's fidelity, or lack thereof, and its repercussions.

Or.

I could make this go away. Protect your mother. Isn't that what Aaron said? Ironically, I'll be protecting my mother from my father, not her boyfriend. Really, it's just a postcard and it could be from anyone and mean anything. Mom might have sent it herself. Yes, that's it. While she was on a trip to Asbury Park which she has since forgotten, Mom sent this postcard to Dad and she happened to be wearing different lipstick. And to make sure that no one else sees this postcard and gets the wrong idea, I tear up the postcard.

Boom. Done. Postcard? What postcard?

See? No therapy required.

Sally, Part Two

Repressing this would go a lot easier if I wasn't standing in the crime scene. I need to get out of the restaurant. I need to drive. Not Sally. Sally belonged to Dad. God only knows what trace evidence I've been driving in.

"Chrissie," I say when I get upstairs. "Switch cars with me for the rest of the weekend. Okay?"

"You're going to let me drive Sally?" he says. "Why?"

"I'm driving to the shore. It's a long trip. She's delicate."

"Take my Subaru," Bette says. "I'll take Sally."

"No."

Bette blinks at my tone. "Okay, hon. I'm just offering. My car is reliable and—"

"Chrissie? Do you want the Mustang or not?"

"Okay, krimpet." Christopher reaches into his pants pocket and hands me his car keys. "You take the Von Hechtmobile. I'll take Sally. It's not an even swap, but . . ."

I'm already out the door.

A Man for All Seasons

In the Von Hechtmobile—a suitably unsexy Honda—I drive out of the parking lot and onto the busy highway. Where am I going? I don't know.

After a series of turns, I merge on a long stretch of quiet road lined with trees and empty fields of grass browned by the summer sun. I pass a horse farm and a farm stand and head toward Westfield. I want to talk to Joe.

Using my cell phone, I call Hunter Farm's office. The machine answers. It's Friday night. Joe wouldn't be in his office. But maybe he's home. I don't have his home phone number. But I'm half a mile away from the farm. I decide to go.

The farm is alive with activity. It's seven o'clock and the sun is just beginning to set. Workers stand in the fields with baskets, pulling tomatoes from their vines. Walking past the first row of plants, I see that squash have replaced the strawberries.

"Mimi?" Turning, I see Joe approaching. He is dirty and disheveled. "What are you doing here? And what the heck are you driving?"

"It's the Von Hechtmobile."

"The what?" Joe laughs.

I say, "Can we talk?"

Joe looks me up and down, and I realize that while my pink skirt and ruffled white top are appropriate for Friday night at Café Louis followed by a birthday party in Avalon—which is where I am supposed to be—my clothes look rather out of place here. Joe smiles and says, "Let's go over there." He points toward the cornfield.

In my two-inch mules, I follow Joe through the dirt to a row of cornstalks. The corn is higher than my head. At eye level are corncobs sheathed in green husks. The cobs stand erect at eighty-degree angles. Black and blond silk tangles at their tips. "Could this be any more phallic?" I ask.

Joe smiles, leans forward, and kisses me. By the time my shock passes, his tongue is in my mouth. I push him away. "What are you doing?"

"I'm kissing you," Joe says.

"I came here to talk."

"Right," Joe says. "You're here on a Friday night dressed like that. To talk."

He thinks I'm here for nooky. I put my hands on my hips and glare at Joe. From my expression, he sees that his assumption was incorrect. Joe looks embarrassed, then annoyed. "You can't just show up here and expect me to drop everything and talk to you." Joe runs his hand through his hair. "End of summer is one of my busiest times."

"Well, then," I say. "I guess you're not a man for all seasons."

◧═▭ ACE East

Joe has disqualified himself. Better go find Aaron.

I drive the Von Hechtmobile south on Route 295, then merge onto the Atlantic City Expressway going east. I still have more than an hour's drive. Blaring the radio doesn't shut out my thoughts.

My family. My childhood. Do I cling to my faux mustard memories, or find the truth? I could ask Bette. Would she confess? What would I do with the truth if I found it?

My father. Who was he, really? If I don't know who he was, how can I know who I am? Look at what I'm doing right this minute. Leaving one man to go to another.

How much like my father am I?

◧═▭ Happy Birthday, Part One

"It's a freakin' mansion" is my observation when Aaron meets me in front of his family's house. All thoughts of my family disappear. I am blinded by this castle by the sea.

Hues of blue and white decorate the large family room. Walking through it, I come to the kitchen, tricked out in stainless-steel, state-of-the-art appliances. The kitchen leads to an enclosed patio on which sits a large wicker dining table topped with glass. It's all very casual and tasteful, but obviously expensive.

Pointing through the patio's glass doors, I ask, "That's the pool?"

"Yeah." Aaron acknowledges the pool nonchalantly, like it isn't an Olympic-sized swimming pool with a five-foot-high, stone waterfall. A Jacuzzi sits next to the pool, as do two cabanas, many chaise longue chairs, and a full bar. A crowd of thirty thirty-somethings fills the pool area. Every one of them is tan, well groomed, and stylishly attired.

"Those are Amanda's friends," Aaron says.

"I don't have thirty friends."

"You missed dinner," he tells me. "But you're just in time for presents, cake, and champagne."

"I didn't bring a present."

"Don't worry about it," Aaron says.

"I can't believe I came to a birthday party without a present. That's not like me. I don't do that kind of thing."

"Look at all those gifts." Aaron gestures to a pretty pile of presents. "Amanda won't notice that you didn't bring a gift."

On the air-conditioned porch, some people sit on upholstered wicker furniture while others stand in a semicircle around the birthday girl as she opens her gifts.

"I'm an idiot," I say quietly.

"Stop, Mimi. You're making a big deal out of nothing."

And why am I doing that? Because there is a bigger deal that I am ignoring. A bigger deal about which I feel similarly helpless.

Amanda unwraps her first few gifts, leaving debris of wrapping paper, ribbon, and tissue paper. People ooh and aah over the presents and press closer to see them. The air on the porch becomes warm, then hot. Sweat beads in my bra and on my forehead, but I smile and nod along with this bunch of strangers.

"Are you okay?" Aaron whispers in my ear.

"It's a little warm. I didn't eat dinner."

Oh, and my father may have cheated on my mother.

Aaron pulls me backward, out of the crowd. Into my ear, he whispers, "Let's get out of here. Want to walk to the beach?"

"Yes, please."

Out the porch door we quietly go. When we pass the poolside bar, Aaron grabs a bottle of champagne.

Young Woman and the Sea

Swiftly we walk down the beach, away from the house. It's dark, but there is light from other houses along the shore. When we are a quarter of a mile away from Aaron's house, he stops. "How's this?"

"Fine." I stand and face the dark ocean. I breathe deeply and feel the silence.

"Did something bad happen today?" Aaron says.

I turn to Aaron. He looks so open. So concerned. "What would you do if you discovered a family secret?"

"Is it a life or death secret?" Aaron asks. "Like, is someone's life in jeopardy?"

"No. It's a secret about something that happened years ago."

"How do you know it's still a secret?" Aaron says.

I look at him. "I didn't know about it."

Aaron shrugs. "That doesn't mean other people don't know."

"I can't ask people if they know or not. That would be giving it away."

"Would it hurt or help people to know the secret?" Aaron asks.

"Hurt. Lots of hurt."

"Then I think you should keep the secret," Aaron says. "Every family has them."

Indeed.

"Can I help?" Aaron asks.

Of course not. But since he is so available, why not tell him one of my many problems? "Sid proposed to my mother."

Aaron doesn't say, "How do you feel about it?" or "Everything will be all right." Aaron doesn't say anything. He stands still and looks at me. And because he doesn't do or say anything, because he is simply standing there, ready to listen, I talk.

"I came home, to what I thought was home, and nothing is the way I thought it would be. And now that I know this secret, I think nothing ever was the way I thought it was. My parents aren't who I thought they were. So who does that make me?"

I don't want to say any more. So I kick off my mules, and wade into the ocean. I go up to my knees, and the water touches the hem of my dress. The roar of the waves is loud, but not loud enough to silence the thoughts in my head.

From behind me, two strong arms circle my waist. I stand up straight, leaning backward against Aaron's chest. With one arm still around my waist, Aaron puts the other arm across my shoulders. For what seems like forever, Aaron holds me against him, supporting me, letting me face the ocean.

I remember Joe swimming into the ocean and screaming at things I couldn't see. And so I scream. I scream frustration, disappointment, and grief. Then I cry. It's been a long time since I cried. I didn't cry over Nick's cheating. But I'm crying over Dad's.

When my tears stop flowing, I take Aaron's hand, and lead him to the shore. We sit on the sand. Aaron says, "What you said about not knowing who your parents are? I think you do know. They loved you and raised you as best they could. What you find out after the fact doesn't change that. Now we're adults and we make our own decisions.

"When I started working at SHRED, I learned things about the company that I wish I didn't know. And that company is old. My great grandfather started it. I decided not to turn my back on my family's company. That's why I worked so hard to establish a residential division of SHRED. So I could do things my way. My dad understood that it was the best way to maintain our relationship. And it's working. I'm making it sound easy, but it took me all of my twenties to realize this."

"I wish I could get a do-over for my twenties," I say. "I wasted them."

With a big pop, Aaron uncorks the champagne bottle. A

little stream of white smoke emerges. He raises the bottle. "Here's to our thirties."

"I'm not off to a great start," I say. But I accept the champagne bottle, take a long swig, then give it back to him.

⊕━━⊑ *Happy Birthday, Part Two*

When I open my eyes, I realize I'm lying on my back. I've been sleeping. I sit up, look down, and see that Aaron is asleep. What time is it? I can't see my watch in the dark.

"Aaron," I say, and shake his arm gently. He doesn't move. "Aaron?" Bending over him, I look at Aaron's face.

He has been so wonderful to me. Not just tonight, but especially tonight. Leaning down, I gently put my mouth on his, then pull away and look at Aaron's face. His eyes are still closed. I close my eyes and kiss him again, more firmly. When I open my eyes, Aaron's eyes are open. I gasp in surprise. Looking back down at Aaron, I see that he is smiling. I kiss him again. And again.

We kiss and roll around on the beach. We get covered in sand. From head to toe, in our hair, ears, and clothes. Laughing, Aaron says, "This looks so hot in the movies."

"But it's kind of gross," I say.

Rolling off me, Aaron gets to his feet and pulls me to mine. Hand in hand, we walk back to his house.

We stand near Aaron's pool, under the lights of the porch, and laugh at ourselves. Our clothes and faces are smeared with sand. "Ssshhh." Aaron gestures to the darkened house. "Everyone is asleep."

"We can't track this sand through your house. Do you have an outdoor shower?"

The Scheins' outdoor shower is against the side of the house and enclosed on three sides. Despite the fact that this outdoor shower is like all others, Aaron and I stand staring at it, unsure what to do. Finally Aaron says, "I'll go first."

"Okay," I say.

"I'm going to take my clothes off," Aaron says.

"Okay." I turn and look elsewhere, but I hear Aaron take off his shorts and shirt. I hear the shower door open, and thinking he is inside, I face forward and catch a glimpse of Aaron's bare back and butt.

We've got to hit that, the diva says.

Slowly. I want to go . . .

Get me some of that, the diva says.

I think the diva is drunk. I listen to her anyway.

Leaving my dress in a pile on the ground, but still wearing my bra and panties, I open the shower door. Aaron turns and looks at me with surprise. I step inside what is essentially a closet, and shut the door.

"Is the water warm?" I ask.

Aaron nods and steps aside, out of the shower stream. I step into the water, and feel the grimy sand wash down my body. I look at Aaron. He is looking at my body, but standing with his back flat against the wall, as far away from me as possible.

Make the first move, the diva says.

Why should I have to?

You've pushed him away too many times, the diva says.

But I'm standing here half naked, under the water, in the dark. Hello?

The diva says, Reach out to him.

I do. I reach out my hand, put it on Aaron's shoulder, and draw him to me. Skin to skin, we stand under the shower kissing and moving our hands over our bodies. Within seconds, Aaron is hard against my belly.

Keep going, the diva says.

There is a narrow bench along the shower wall, which I find accidentally by kicking my leg against it. I sit on the bench and pull Aaron toward me.

But I get cold fast. When a breeze blows against the side of the house and into the shower, I shiver. Which Aaron can't help but notice, given the position we're in. "Do you want to go inside?" he asks.

"Yes," I say.

Aaron and I tiptoe up the grand staircase. Aaron looks toward the guest wing. All is quiet, all is dark. Aaron leads me down the hallway of the guest wing, and I wonder where the heck he's going. Aaron comes to a stop outside the bedroom. "You can sleep in this guest room."

What? the diva shouts.

I can't see Aaron's face in the dark, but I feel him lean toward me. "Good night," he whispers in my ear, and kisses my cheek.

No way, the diva states.

Taking Aaron's hand, I lead him down the hall toward his room.

Sometime around dawn, the diva says, Happy birthday.

◼━◻ ACE West

"I thought you were going to spend the weekend," Aaron said.

"I have to work," I answered.

I replay the conversation as I drive the Von Hechtmobile along the Garden State Parkway and look for the sign to the Atlantic City Expressway West.

"Stay for breakfast, Mimi."

"I don't want to get stuck in traffic."

Every Jerseyan knows that there is no westbound traffic on a Saturday morning.

"I hope you don't regret what we did last night," Aaron said.

"Not at all."

The memory of last night makes the diva open her eyes and stretch. In response, I drive my car faster.

"I didn't mean to . . ." Aaron left his sentence unfinished.

"Everything is fine," I said. "But I really have to go."

You handled that well, the diva says.

Don't talk while I'm driving. And haven't you gotten us into enough trouble?

Not nearly, the diva says. But I must say, we've made better exits. Don't you think we owed Aaron a proper goodbye? Morning sex can be lovely.

We didn't have sex.

Orgasms were had, the diva laughs.

But we didn't have intercourse.

Don't try to Clinton your way out of this, the diva says.

I'm not in love with Aaron.

So what? the diva asks. Since when do you have to be in love with someone to hook up with him, have fun, and make me happy? Anyway, who says he's in love with you? Me, he's quite fond of. But you? After this morning, he might not like you at all.

I made a mistake.

"I made a mistake," I tell Madeline over my cell as I merge onto ACE West.

"Finally," she says.

"What?"

"Mimi, you've been so careful all summer. It's about time you made a mistake. What'd you do?"

"I hooked up with Aaron," I say.

Madeline is quiet for a few moments. "And?"

"And I shouldn't have."

"It was bad?" Madeline asks, and I realize I am talking to entirely the wrong person about this. Oh, well.

"It wasn't bad," I say.

"Detail me."

"I don't know what to say. It was nice. Warm."

"Warm? That's the only adjective you can come up with? The first time Nick kissed you good night, it took you thirty-four minutes to tell me about it. When you told me about Farmer Joe, you described the texture of his beard, the color of his body hair, the smell of the barn.

Now you're telling me that Aaron was, what did you say? Warm? I guess you did make a mistake."

"That's not what I meant, Maddie. You're making Aaron sound worse than he was."

"Why are you covering for him? Put your diva on the phone."

I laugh. "She's recuperating."

"Ah, well, that's something."

"It was fulfilling, but not terribly exciting. Like tofu."

"Tofu is bland. And you, Mimi Louis, are not a vegetarian. I vote for Joe. Give him another chance. He's got a lot more flavor."

☞ *The Diva Made Me Do It*

Excuses and escapes aside, I do have a valid reason for going to work. I need to exchange the Von Hechtmobile for Sally. And there is a bridal shower brunch at Café Louis and I need to make sure everything is in order.

Which it is, as I see when I arrive at the restaurant. Christopher von Hecht has everything well in hand. Okay, so I'm not needed. I don't want to go home to deal with Mom's impending engagement, and I don't want to watch the brunch party's bridal glee. So I retreat to the downstairs office and obsess just a little more about my steamy sessions with Aaron and Joe. Should I give Joe another chance? Does he want one?

* * *

"What's up, butternut?" Christopher von Hecht smiles as he hands me the credit card receipt for the bridal brunch.

"I made a mistake."

"With the bill?" Christopher leans over my shoulder.

"No. With Joe and Aaron.

"Still caught between two lovers?" he says. "I thought I settled this for you."

"They aren't lovers," I insist. "The mistake is that I insulted Joe and hooked up with Aaron. What was I thinking? Ugh. The diva made me do it."

Christopher sits on my desk. "Made you do . . . what?"

"What matters is that I didn't have sex with Joe or Aaron. And I'm not going to. I want to wait."

"Wait for what?" Christopher asks.

"For my brain to be sure of what my body should do. My last relationship started with sex. And ended with sex. Him having sex with someone else. And you know what? I was on a date with another man when I met Nick. A perfectly nice man. I can't remember his name, but he could have been the love of my life. Did I give him a chance? No, I did not. I got thrusty with Nick."

Christopher tsks. "It happens, patty pan. Don't beat yourself up about it."

"What I'm saying is that I want this time to be different. I spent my twenties dating and having casual sex and where did it get me?"

"It got you to orgasm, I hope."

"Yeah, but then what? I went from boyfriend to boyfriend, bed to bed. Somewhere along the line, the sex became meaningless. Now that I haven't had sex for a few months, it means something again. I like that. Sex should mean something, don't you think?"

"Sure." Christopher raises an eyebrow. "What should it mean?"

"I think it should be . . ." I think for a few moments, then say, "I think it should be a gift. That I give someone. Someone I care about a lot. Until then, I'll wait. For actual intercourse, I mean. Fooling around is still fun. But waiting to do the deed makes me feel good. Empowered."

Christopher smiles. "Abstinence becomes you."

"I almost lost it a few times. It's not easy to stop traffic on the diva highway, you know what I mean?"

"No," Christopher says.

"But Joe and Aaron are definitely in my hookup hall of fame. All that sexual tension building? That's the best part. I love it."

Christopher laughs. "Ain't lust grand?"

"Mom? I'm home. Mom? Mom!" The sound of *The Sound of Music* soundtrack leads me to the kitchen. No wonder Mom can't hear me. Whatever. Must pee.

As I tinkle, I hum along with the music to "Sixteen Going on Seventeen." I never cared for Rolf. What kind of name is Rolf?

"Mom?" Walking past the stereo en route to the kitchen, I turn down the volume. "Mom, you shouldn't listen to music so loudly that you can't hear anything else. Someone could break in and you'd be none the wiser." I walk into the kitchen.

My mother is sprawled on the kitchen floor. Her eyes are closed.

◼━◁ *Bobbi Louis, Part Two*

First, I do nothing. Mom lies on the floor and I stare at her. She's wearing a housedress. An old one. The dress is bunched around her thighs. A cleaning rag lies near her head. Fumes, I think. She passed out from the Pledge. No. That doesn't happen.

Then I do something ridiculous. I try to make a deal with whatever higher power may be listening.

Don't let her be dead, I think. I'll do anything.

No one answers me.

For no good reason, I get on my knees and crawl to my mother. I'm afraid to touch her. I don't want her body to be cold. "Mom?" I say quietly. I look at her chest. It's moving up and down. She's breathing.

I take Mom's hand and pat it. What am I doing? Do I think this will revive her? Telephone, I think. I have to call 911. Then, Mom's eyes flutter open. "Oh," she says. Mom turns her face to me.

"Mom? What happened?"

"Oh," she says again. She plants her free hand on the floor and tries to sit up.

"Don't move," I say. "You may have a neck injury."

"What?" Mom says.

"That's what they say on TV. I'm calling 911. Don't move."

"Mimi, I'm fine. Really. I got dizzy and, I don't know. I guess I fell. I'm fine."

But I'm already dialing the phone. My emergency, I tell the dispatcher, is that I found my mother unconscious on the floor. Yes, she's breathing. Yes, she's awake now. Yes, I absolutely want an ambulance to come.

"Ambulance?" Mom says. "Don't be ridiculous."

"They'll be here in three minutes," I tell her, hanging up the phone.

"Good God, Mimi. My doctor switched my blood pressure medication. I'm sure that's the cause of this. I'm fine." Indeed, she sits up, but she winces.

"I told you not to move," I say, crouching down to her.

"I bruised something. Call them back and tell them not to come."

"They're coming," I say.

"Well, then, get me some underwear."

"Excuse me?"

"I'm not wearing any underwear. Get a pair from my dresser, will you?"

Without asking why my mother was cleaning the house sans underwear, I go quickly to her room and grab a pair of panties. "Not those," she says when I return to the kitchen. "Get a pair of nice ones."

I stare at Mom.

She says, "I can't go to the hospital wearing bad underwear."

For lack of a coherent statement, I say, "Okay."

When I return to the kitchen, Mom is lying on the floor, awaiting her panties. She shimmies them up her legs, lifts her tush, and puts on her panties. "Do I have time to put on my makeup?" she asks.

I stare at her, speechless.

"At least get me some lipstick," she says.

Fifteen minutes later, Mom is en route to the hospital. Without her lipstick. I follow in my car. The EMT guys said that Mom's vitals are fine, but nonetheless strapped her into a gurney. "This is so embarrassing," Mom said as they carried her out of the house.

I call my brother's house. Jeremy answers. And for some reason, I ask to speak to Allison. I tell her exactly what happened. "We'll meet you at the hospital," she says succinctly, and hangs up the phone.

Twenty minutes later, Mom is in a curtained area in the ER of South Jersey Hospital. She has several doohickeys attached to her chest and arms. Monitoring her heart rate, the doctor told me. Blood has been taken. Tests are being run. And my mother keeps complaining about her lipstick. "I look like a mess," Mom says. "Give me some of your lipstick. It's not the right color for me but it's better than nothing."

"I don't have my purse," I tell her.

"Why did you leave the house without your purse?" Mom asks.

"Because, Mom, you were passed out on the freaking floor."

Just then, the curtain draws back and I see Allison, with Jeremy standing behind her.

"Mom," Allison says, and comes forward to take Mom's hand. Jeremy, however, stands still and stares at Mom.

"Jeremy, I'm fine," Mom says.

But Jeremy's eyes well with tears.

"Jeremy," Mom says loudly. "I'm okay, honey."

Tears run out of Jeremy's eyes, and the sight of my brother crying makes my own eyes wet. I know what he sees. Not our mother, but our father.

"Mrs. Louis," says the doctor as he appears at the foot of her bed.

Mom and Allison say, "Yes?"

"Sorry," the doctor says. He points at Mom. "That Mrs. Louis."

"These are my children," Mom says. Infused with unnecessary formality, Mom introduces each of us. Jeremy wipes his eyes and shakes the doctor's hand.

"Okay," the doctor says. "Your tests are fine, Mrs. Louis. I spoke to your doctor. She agrees that your fainting was due to the switch in your high blood pressure mediation."

Jeremy frowns. "Why didn't you tell us that the doctor switched your medication?"

"It's not a big deal," Mom says.

"I want to know everything," Jeremy says.

"Do you want to hear about my Pap smear?" Mom says. Jeremy winces.

"The high blood pressure medication caused abnormal excitation of your vagus nerve and slowed the rate of your heartbeat," the doctor says. "The medical term is vasovagal syncope. Or, fainting."

"How Scarlett of you," I say to Mom.

Jeremy says, "You think this is funny, Mimi?"

"No," I say and look at my shoes.

"Doctor," Mom says. "Could you prescribe some sedatives for my children?"

The doctor says, "I consulted with your doctor and we're going to switch medications. You should take it easy for the next few days to make sure there are no other side effects. Luckily, you didn't break or sprain anything. But you have a large contusion on your right buttock."

"I have a bruised butt?" Mom says.

The doctor smiles. "You'll feel some soreness in your lower back. Ibuprofen will help with that. If you can manage it, staying off your feet for a few days is a good idea. You don't want to further strain your back."

"She'll stay with us," Allison says.

"I'll be fine," Mom says.

"She will absolutely stay with us," Jeremy tells the doctor.

"I can take care of myself," Mom says.

"No," Jeremy and Allison say in unison.

"Hello? I live with her," I say. "I can take care of her."

"Excuse me," Mom says. "I want to go home."

●━━◀═ *Home*

"Leave me alone," Mom says.

Jeremy, Allison, and I stand around Mom's bed. We have been arguing about how best to care for Mom, when the truth is that there is nothing to do. She is fine, for the most part. "I'd like to take a nap," Mom says, "if that's okay with all of you."

"Mom," I say. "Do you want me to call Sid?"

"No."

Why not? Because she doesn't want to worry him? Because she doesn't want Sid to see her like this? Because she turned down his marriage proposal? Now is not the time to ask these questions. Or any of the others that lurk in the back of my brain.

Jeremy stands in Mom's kitchen with his hands on his hips. "When Mom wakes up, we'll pack her a bag and move her to our house."

"She wants to stay here," I say.

"I don't care what she wants," Jeremy says. "Do you know what could have happened to her?"

"I'll be here," I say.

"Where were you when she fell? Why didn't you know that her blood pressure medication had changed? Why didn't you go to the doctor with her last week? Because you had to work at the restaurant, right? You know what, Mimi? Your priorities are really screwed up."

"Hey," Allison says. She puts her hand on Jeremy's arm.

"It's okay," I say. "He's not completely wrong."

"I know he's not wrong," Allison says. "I think he's right. But you should go outside so you don't disturb you mother."

Into Mom's garden we go. Jeremy folds his arms over his chest. "You've spent the whole summer putting that restaurant before your family," Jeremy says. "You're just like Dad."

"I am not like Dad."

Jeremy squints at me. "You've always been like Dad. Loving the restaurant business. I've always been like Mom. Taking care of my family. And if something happens to Mom . . ."

Jeremy gets tears in his eyes. He blinks furiously.

". . . then I don't know what I would do. I mean, I think about it a lot. Mom's in good shape, but eventually her health is going to deteriorate. You know how many other people her age are already dealing with serious illnesses?"

Grammy Jeff. Mrs. Hunter. "Yes."

Jeremy keeps going. "You want to start your own family? Try taking care of the family you have. This is what it means to be an adult and have adult responsibilities."

"Listen, Jeremy, I realize you're freaked out by this, but you can stop yelling at me. I have responsibilities. Not as many as you, but I have them. Now that I know what the situation is with Mom, I will be more attentive to her. Okay?"

My brother swallows. He starts to blink furiously. Is he crying?

"I'm sorry to yell at you. It's just . . . We've already lost one parent, Mimi. And today, in the hospital? I looked at Mom in that hospital bed and I thought . . ." Jeremy puts his hands over his eyes.

Allison, who must have been watching from the kitchen window, comes rushing into the garden. She wraps her arms around Jeremy's waist. Jeremy bends over Allison, resting his head on hers. "I'm here," she says. Jeremy lets loose a sob.

For a moment, I stand and watch my brother cry on his

wife. Then I turn and leave them alone. I go to my room and sit on my bed.

If something happened to Mom . . .

She's the parent I have left and she's a super fantastic woman. For so many years, I have been daddy's little girl. Now?

I want my mommy.

☞ *Mothers, Part Two*

Jeremy finally agrees to "let" Mom stay in her own home. Before he and Allison leave to rescue their kids from Phoebe, Jeremy spends twenty minutes with Mom in her room. With the door shut.

Mom sleeps straight through the night. So do I. The next morning, I call the restaurant and tell Grammy Jeff that I won't be at work for a few days. I don't tell Grammy about Mom's fainting drama because I don't want her to worry.

"We'll take care of the restaurant," Grammy says. "You take a few days to relax."

Right.

"My butt hurts," Mom says when I bring her breakfast in bed. It's only scrambled eggs, toast, and fruit, but Mom acts as if I've created a masterpiece. "You didn't have to go to all this trouble. And you don't have to babysit me all day. You have things to do."

"Consider today a belated Mother's Day," I say.

Mom and I spend the morning icing her butt, watching talk shows, and flipping through fashion magazines.

"You haven't asked me about Sid," Mom says as she eats the grilled cheese sandwich I made for lunch.

"I thought you'd tell me when you were ready," I say.

"I'm not going to marry Sid," Mom says.

"May I ask why not?"

"I enjoy my life the way it is," Mom says. "I like my freedom."

"You can't be free with Sid? Were you free with Dad?"

Mom thinks for a few moments. "Your father was always so busy with the restaurant. And that was okay with me."

"It was?" I say.

"Oh, yes. Don't get me wrong. I loved your father. I just didn't want him around the house all the time."

"Really?"

"Sure. I got to spend more time with you and Jeremy and not worry about making the dinner my husband wanted and having it on the table at a certain time. Remember our Sunday dinners? That was the only day of the week we all sat down together at the table. And that was fine with me."

"We would spend Sundays together," I say, remembering.

"Your father and I would spend Mondays together," Mom says. "While you and Jeremy were at school."

"Really?"

"Oh, yes. All day." She wiggles her eyebrows at me.

"Enough," I say. "Yuck."

But if Dad was having sexcapades with Mom, maybe he

didn't need to look for outside entertainment. Maybe she is the B on the postcard.

"The issue with Sid is that he is retired and he hasn't found ways to occupy his time," Mom says. "He's been very dependent on me. I already have my own things that I love to do. So I told Sid all of this. Every last bit of it. And he agreed that he needs to fill his life with things other than me. He needs to be more independent. So, we'll keep dating and see what happens."

"And the ring?" I say.

"Sid said I could keep the ring."

"Okay," I say. "Let freedom ring."

What rings is the doorbell. "That's Maddie," I tell Mom. "I told her about yesterday's drama and she insisted on coming over when she was finished with work."

Wearing a black tank top and baggy white pants, Madeline says, "How is she?" when I open the door.

"She's fine." I reach for the pink Tiers box Madeline holds.

"No." Madeline swats at my hands. "This is for Bobbi."

"It's a cheesecake," Madeline tells Mom as she hands over the Tiers box. "I don't know how to make chicken soup. I thought this would be the next best thing."

"That's very sweet," Mom says. "Thank you."

I take the cake box to the kitchen and cut three slices. Plates in hand, I return to Mom's room. Madeline has wrapped her arms around my mother. Mom rubs Madeline's back. I stand in the doorway and watch, not wanting to interrupt. After a few moments, Madeline separates herself from Mom.

"Thanks," Madeline says. "I needed that."

━━━◄ *Jobs*

Christopher von Hecht calls my cell. "Listen, boss girl. I know you are on holiday, but I have to tell you something serious."

"What?"

"I found a new job, so I'm officially giving you two weeks' notice."

"What? Why?"

"Don't be mad, okay? Business has been so slow. I hope you understand."

I do understand. It's pretty simple. He needs to make money. "Where are you going?" I ask.

"Habanero Grill," Christopher sighs.

"A chain?" I say. "Chrissie, I can get you a better job than that."

"You can?" he says.

"Listen, Brussels sprout. I opened five restaurants in Philadelphia last year. I'm sure one of them is looking to hire an experienced waiter. Give me a few hours."

Why should I call five different restaurants when I can go straight to Dine International? I call the office and the new receptionist tells me that Claire McKenzie is on vacation. Not wanting to keep Christopher von Hecht in limbo, I ask to speak with Peter Exter.

"Hello, stranger," my former boss greets me.

I tell him the purpose for my call, and Peter tells me that

Dine International is opening a new American restaurant in Philadelphia. If Christopher Von Hecht is as good as I say he is, Peter will hire him right now. "Consider it done," Peter says. "I don't suppose you want to come back to work for me."

"You're hiring?"

"Mimi, you never even asked me for your job back. You just blew out of town."

"Oh. That's true. But you had just hired Claire. It wouldn't be fair to fire her."

"I would have found something for you to do," Peter says. "You're too valuable a commodity, Mimi."

"Thank you," I say.

"In fact, we are looking for someone to headhunt chefs for us in Europe. We're opening restaurants in London and Florence, and another one in Paris. It's a month-long assignment. Tempted?"

"Thank you, but no," I say. "I don't want to travel anymore. I want to stay close to my family."

"I'm going to start looking for an apartment," I tell Mom as we watch HGTV.

"Maybe you can get your old apartment back," Mom suggests.

"Not in Philadelphia. Here. Not in The Garden, but somewhere in South Jersey."

"Why?" Mom says.

"Why? Why else? To be near you. And the rest of the family."

"And the restaurant?"

"Yes," I say.

"By the way," Mom says. "I called the towns I know and I couldn't find a shore house for us to stay in during the last week of August. Maybe we could take a few day trips. Unless you still want to investigate Asbury Park?"

"No."

◼━━◗ *Mothers, Part Three*

We have to get through the farewell dinner for Phoebe and her Latin lover. "Do I have to go?" Mom says. "I'm feeling dizzy."

"Nice try," I tell her. "Get in the car."

Over dessert of pound cake and fruit, Jeremy says, "We have an announcement to make. Allison is pregnant."

"Mazel tov, mazel tov!" Phoebe claps her hands, then leans toward Allison and kisses both her cheeks. Mom rises, too, and hugs Jeremy. Phoebe continues to kiss Allison, not releasing her grip on her, so Mom leans forward and kisses Allison's head.

"Congratulations," Enrique says as he shakes Jeremy's hand and offers Allison a broad smile.

"How far along are you?" Mom asks.

"Six weeks," Allison says. "The doctor called this morning to confirm it. It's still early, but I wanted to tell everyone while Mom was here."

Getting to my feet, I hug Jeremy. "Congratulations, big daddy."

"Thanks." He returns my squeeze. "We have more news. We'll need another bedroom. So we're going to buy a new house."

Oy. More money.

I return to my seat while the conversation turns to the real estate market. In my seat, I turn to Sarah. "You've lived in this house all of your life. How do you feel about moving?"

Sarah shrugs. "It's what is best for my family."

I nod. We sit quietly for a few moments, watching the rest of the family. Sarah is so like Allison, keeping her feelings to herself. I ask, "What do you think about your mother being pregnant?"

Sarah answers, "I hope it's not twins."

"You be a good girl," Phoebe says as she kisses my cheeks. "You'll find a good man."

"Let's hope."

Mom and I drive home quietly. She doesn't share her thoughts about Allison's pregnancy. I don't share my thoughts about the restaurant. Jeremy needs money, even though he doesn't know I know. So, either I work ten times harder to make Café Louis profitable, or I sell the restaurant. What is best for the family?

◼▭◁ *The Language of Heaven*

Thunder wakes me. Opening my eyes, I see my niece standing by my bed. "Good morning, Aunt Mimi," she says.

211

"What are you doing here? Is something wrong?"

"I'm spending the day with Bubbie," Sarah says. "But it's about to rain and this bed is the best place to watch storms."

"Oh." My adrenaline ebbs as I make room for Sarah. She climbs onto my bed, sits on her knees, and folds her arms on the windowsill. Sarah puts her face against the closed window, her nose almost touching the pane. "I think storms are beautiful," Sarah says.

"The lightning and thunder don't scare you?" I ask.

"Oh, no. They're beautiful. I love when the thunder booms really loud."

Such an odd and beautiful child she is. "Why do you like thunder?"

Sarah inclines her head, watching the dark clouds gather and listening to rumbling thunder. "I pretend the thunder is Grandpa and Zadie talking to each other in heaven."

I ask, "What do Grandpa and Zadie talk about?"

"Lots of stuff."

"And you hear them? They speak real words? In English?"

Sarah smiles. "I think everyone speaks the same language in heaven. You can hear them, too. You just have to listen."

Thunder booms, lightning cracks. The storm arrives.

◼━◔ *Deconstructing Mimi*

After three days of nursing Mom and her sore butt, I drive to Café Louis not having made a decision about the restaurant's future. It's just that . . .

"What is going on?" I shout out the window as I park Sally.

"Demolition," a hard-hatted man tells me.

Debris stands in piles around Café Louis. Yellow trucks bearing red and purple SHRED logos stand guard while an enormous wrecking ball crashes into the remains of the shops that were once Café Louis's neighbors.

"You're pissed off at me so you send in the wrecking crew?" I'm shouting at Aaron through my cell phone.

"First of all," Aaron says, "I'm not pissed off at you. Second, the demolition was scheduled weeks ago."

"So this has nothing to do with me leaving you at the shore?"

"No," Aaron says in a calm voice. "You said that you had to work. Was that a lie?"

"No."

"You know what, Mimi? I like you. I like spending time with you. But I've had it with this back-and-forth crap. I was perfectly willing to take things slowly between us, but you came into the outdoor shower to be with me. I didn't pressure you. Then you bolted in the morning, like I had done something wrong. Which I didn't."

"No, you didn't. Aaron, I'm just . . ."

"Listen, Mimi. I've tried to be patient and supportive. I thought we had a good thing going. Or starting to go. But you need to decide what you want. When you do, let me know."

"Okay, Aaron, I understand . . ." But he's already hung up his phone.

Grammy Love, Part Three

Grammy Jeff stands at the back door of Café Louis. She holds a glass of iced tea. A pile of empty white packets sits on the counter next to her spoon.

"Quite a ruckus," she says. She sips her tea calmly, as if she's looking at a cornfield instead of a battlefield. I stand next to her at the door. "Who were you yelling at on your phone?"

"Aaron Schein."

"Did it make you feel better?" Grammy asks.

"No."

Grammy nods.

I say, "I'm going to sell Café Louis."

"I know," Grammy says. "I knew all summer. I was just waiting for you to say it out loud."

"Well, now I've said it. It's not just because of the construction. Jeremy's wife is pregnant. Again. And they could use the money from the sale to buy a new house."

"I think that would make your daddy happy," Grammy says.

"Closing the restaurant would make him happy?" I say.

"Sure. Put the money to good use. Help the family. I think that Jay's biggest regret was not living long enough to tie up his loose ends."

"What loose ends?" I say.

"Oh, you know. Put money aside for the grandkids. Make sure your mamma was settled right. And he'd want to have taken care of his restaurant family, too. Help everyone get a new job. Like you did for Christopher. That was good."

"But I failed. I came here to keep the restaurant open."

Grammy shrugs. "Maybe you came here to close it. The right way."

□══╡ *Eat Your Peas*

Madeline and I sit on metal stools, staring out the back door of the restaurant. The wrecking ball has come and gone, leaving massive piles of debris.

"So you're going to sell the restaurant," Madeline says.

"Yes."

"That will make Aaron happy."

I say, "I don't think so. He's had it with me."

"And Farmer Joe?" Madeline says.

"I freaked at him a few days ago."

"So you've pissed off both of them?"

"Yep," I confirm.

"Nicely done," Madeline says.

"Thank you."

We sit quietly until Madeline says, "I'll be happy to hire the San Padre brothers. It sounds like they are hard workers. They can bake?"

"Bake. Cook. They can do anything."

"Can they wait until I get back? I'm taking a week's vacation from Tiers."

"Where are you going?" I ask.

"To see my mother." Madeline stares at the demolition. "Seeing you work out your family issues has got me thinking about my family issues."

"Such as?"

"Well, Mimi, you may not have noticed but I have some problems with men and relationships. It is possible that I have some residual crap from my parents' divorce. I thought all that stuff was buried. But I think the ghost of it is haunting me. You know?"

"I do know. I really do, Maddie."

"I'm going to spend the week with my mom. See what we can talk through."

"Are you sure you want to do that? If there's one thing I've learned this summer, it's that every family has secrets. Things we had no idea existed because our parents wanted to do what's best for us. Like when they made us eat asparagus by bribing us with dessert. Or, they hid peas in our mashed potatoes and thought we wouldn't notice. But eventually, we find the peas."

Madeline smiles. "Or maybe life is like a meal. You can't fully appreciate dessert until you eat your peas."

⚼ *Menu Theory*

After Madeline leaves, I sit in the downstairs office. Closing Café Louis is the right thing to do. But it makes me sad. Looking around the office, I think about packing it up for good. There's just so much crap. Do I need any of it? No.

What do I need? I came to Café Louis looking for a part of myself that I thought I had lost. My optimism. My love of the restaurant business. I have found them here. I take them with me.

And I take my father with me, wherever I go. The good is good. The bad? Do I need to eat my peas? Or can I select a different side dish? Can I pick and choose which family dishes, which of my family's legacies, I want?

Maybe families are like menus. There's Dad's work ethic. His creativity. Mom's love of life. Love of love. Jeremy's devotion to his family. To Mom. Allison? She's a side dish, but a savory one. She believes in marriage and motherhood. Even Sid is on the menu. He has restored my faith in romanticism. He has made me appreciate the art of woo.

Joe or Aaron? It's no wonder I can't decide on a dessert. My entrée needs more cooking. Maybe I need to blend and balance my own flavors before I add someone else's.

Of course, this could all be a bunch of bunk.

✎ *Family Business, Part Four*

"I thought we were doing something fun," Sarah says as we park Sally in front of Café Louis.

"We are doing something fun," I say.

Sarah looks at me doubtfully. "Mom said this place is getting torn down."

"It is. Soon. But not today. Today, it's our restaurant. Yours and mine."

Sarah peers at Café Louis. "It looks old and dirty."

"Maybe," I say. "But inside, she's magic."

Sarah follows me to the concrete steps leading to the restaurant. "Remember earlier this summer, when you said that the restaurant is more important than you?"

Sarah nods.

"I don't want you to feel that way. This restaurant is part of our family, Sarah. I want you to see Café Louis the way I saw her when I was your age. We'll have to use a little imagination, but I think we have plenty of that. What do you say?"

"Okay," Sarah says.

SHRED is holding an auction tomorrow to sell as much of Café Louis as possible. The restaurant was scrubbed clean yesterday. This morning, the sun sparkles through the windows as Sarah and I walk into the dining room. "What do you smell?" I ask Sarah.

Sarah sticks her nose in the air. "Sunshine."

"Oh, look," I say. "Here's our first customer."

Sarah looks at the door. "No one is there."

"Mr. and Mrs. Raspberry. How nice to see you." I walk through the room holding two menus. "Your waitress Sarah will be with you in a moment."

Sarah smiles. I lead her to the waiters' station and tie a short, black apron around her waist. Handing her an ordering pad, I say, "Ask Mr. and Mrs. Raspberry what they would like to eat for lunch. Write it down on the pad. Oh, and look. The Watermelon sisters just walked in the door. You'll have to wait on them next. I'll put the menus down, then you take their order. Okay?"

"Okay." Sarah goes to the Raspberry booth. "What would you like to eat?"

She looks back at me. I nod her onward.

"Now we have to cook," I tell Sarah and lead her into the kitchen. I remove her black apron and tie a white one around her. "Do you cook with your mother?"

Sarah shakes her head. "I watch her cook sometimes. But Mom says to stay away from the stove. And the knives."

"She's right," I say. "I'll be the chef. You be the sous chef."

"Okay," she says, although I'm sure she has no idea what a sous chef is.

"What's the first order?" I ask. "What do the Raspberrys want to eat?"

"Hot dogs and spaghetti."

"What do the Watermelon sisters want to eat?" I ask.

"Chicken fingers and coleslaw."

I open the refrigerator. "We don't have that. But I have

an idea. Why don't we make one big dish and give a little bit to everyone?"

Sarah says, "The customers might not like that."

"Sure they will. You know why? We're going to make something very special. Louis family chicken soup." From the refrigerator, I pull ingredients I placed there last night. Chicken stock, which I cooked myself because I thought the carcass might be too much for Sarah. I saw one when I was her age and it turned me vegetarian. For a month.

"Celery, carrots, parsnip, and look at all these herbs." I put the ingredients on the metal worktable. I give Sarah a bunch of parsley. "What does it smell like?"

"Spring," she says.

As I chop and dice, Sarah smells all the herbs and vegetables. I tell her their names in Spanish, English, and French. "Now comes the most important job," I tell Sarah. "Stirring. Can you handle that?"

Sarah nods eagerly. I pull a metal stool next to the stove and lift Sarah onto it. She holds a large wooden spoon and stirs as I add ingredients to the boiling water. Quietly, Sarah sits and concentrates on her stirring. "Cooking is fun, Aunt Mimi."

"Yes, Sarah. Cooking is fun."

▬▬◖ *Family Business, Part Five*

"This is what you want?" Aaron asks.

He stands at Bette's counter wearing a summery beige suit and powder blue shirt. Aaron has come to collect the contracts. I hold the manila folder out to Aaron, but he doesn't take them.

I say, "Selling the restaurant is what's best for my family."

Aaron takes the manila folder.

"I'm sorry, Aaron. I shouldn't have shown you my crazy. The demolition caught me off-guard."

"Your dramatics caught me off-guard."

"I know you think business isn't personal, but it has been an awkward time for us to date," I say. "What with your father's company trying to buy my father's company."

"I guess."

"The thing is, I'm not Juliet. And Chrissie isn't Richard Dawson."

"What?"

"Never mind," I say.

Aaron looks at the floor. "Well, I'm sorry it has to end this way."

"Does it have to end?"

Aaron looks at me. "You don't want it to end?"

"I think we need more time to explore our full potential. I've been preoccupied all summer. With my family and the restaurant. But you have been patient and supportive, like you said. Things are different, or they are going to be different. I do want to take our relationship slowly, but I don't want it to come to a screeching halt."

Aaron smiles. Ah, progress.

"What do you think?" I say.

"I think you're nuts, Mimi."

"For sure."

"But I like nuts." Aaron moves closer to me. "Walnuts. Pecans. Almonds."

"Those are good nuts." I move closer to him. "How about Mimi nuts?"

"They might be an acquired taste." Aaron frowns. "I'd like to keep the nuts to a minimum, though. No more dramatics."

"I can't promise that. But I can promise to mix the nuts with . . ."

Aaron raises his eyebrows and smiles.

I shrug. "I'm all out of metaphor. Seriously, I plan on being much more sane. What I can offer is a lot of sane, some fun, and a minimum amount of drama."

"That's a good deal."

"That's a good deal, too." I point at the contracts. "Thank you."

"You're welcome," Aaron says. "Now that family business is out of the way, should we seal our deal with a kiss?"

"Absolutely." I kiss him.

"So what are you going to do with yourself?" Aaron asks. "Do you have time to run away with me to a sun-drenched island? Or we could hang in Avalon. You need a vacation. After today, I need a vacation."

"I'm not much for islands. But I miss Europe. Actually, my former boss offered me a temporary assignment. One month, four cities. I could turn it into a working holiday. Do you have a passport?"

◼️▬◄ *Jobs, Part Two*

I dial Peter Exter's phone number at Dine International. "I'll take the European job," I tell him. "Your offer is very generous, but there's something else I need."

"Ever the negotiator," Peter says. "What is it?"

"Instead of one airline ticket, I need two."

◼️▬◄ *The Jeffersons*

"We're taking the train?" Nelson asks me as we park Sally in the PATCO lot in Camden.

"It's an easier way to get into Philadelphia." I told Nelson that I needed to pick up the last of my things from Nick's. I asked Nelson to help me. I lied.

Grammy Jeff is leaving tomorrow. She's going to North Carolina, where she goes every year for the week Café Louis is closed. This time, Grammy is spending two weeks with her family. Or three weeks. "Depends how I feel," she said. "And we'll see what the hurricanes do. But I'll come back sooner or later. Nellie needs me. He's my real family."

I helped Grammy pack up her knives and other kitchen tools. "I was thinking the other day," she says, "about your name. Your real name."

"Luvizpharska?"

Grammy looks at me funny.

"Luvitz?"

"Miriam," she says. "Your real name is Miriam. You know who you're named for?"

"My father's cousin."

"No, child. Miriam in the Bible. You know who she was?"

"She was the sister of Moses and Aaron."

"She was a lot more than that," Grammy says. "It was Miriam who followed baby Moses's basket as it floated down the Nile. When Miriam saw the Pharaoh's daughter take the baby's basket, she was very brave and asked the princess if her mother could be the baby's nurse. 'Then said his sister to the Pharaoh's daughter, "Shall I go and call a nurse of the Hebrew women so she may nurse the child for you?" ' The princess agreed. Exodus, two, seven. So, you see? Miriam kept the family together."

Grammy smiled at the perplexed look on my face. She gave me a big, sweet hug and whispered, "I'll be seeing you soon, baby girl."

When we get off the PATCO train at Broad Street, Nelson follows me down the street. I watch him look at the different theaters that line the Avenue of the Arts.

"Here we are." I lead Nelson inside a building.

"We're going into a restaurant?" Nelson asks.

I don't answer, but lead him through the dining room to the kitchen. Nelson's head swivels as he looks at the different cooking stations, the modern equipment, and all the food lying around in different states of readiness. "Nelson," I say. "This is Nicco."

Nelson turns and looks at Nick. Nick smiles. "Nice to meet you, Nelson."

"I've seen you on TV," Nelson says.

Nick nods. "I hear that you're a good cook. Do you want to come work for me?"

Nelson's jaw drops.

"I know you haven't been to culinary school," Nick says. "But you can learn on the job. I'd start you out doing prep work and learning the different terms for cuts. Tournade, chiffonade, all that. If you do well there, I'll move you up through the different cooking stations. Salad, fry, grill. Think of it as an apprenticeship."

"For real?"

"For real, man," Nick says.

Nelson clears his throat. "I'll work real hard for you, Chef."

Nick nods, acknowledging the respectful title. "Can you work nights?" Nick asks. "What time is the last train?"

"I'll start right now, Chef." Nelson starts to take off his coat.

Nick laughs. "Tomorrow is fine. Be here at three o'clock."

"Yes, sir." Nelson offers his hand. "Thank you, Chef."

Nick shakes his hand. "You're welcome."

I turn to Nick. "Thank you, Chef Nicco."

"Thank you, Mimi. For everything."

◼━━🍴 *Accounts Payable*

"Knock, knock," I say as I enter the office at Hunter Farm. It's a wildly hot Saturday afternoon. I step into the office's air-conditioning and shut the door behind me.

"You're not big on calling ahead, are you?" Joe says from his desk.

"I didn't want you to tell me not to come. Or give you a chance to hide."

Joe sorts papers on his desk. "What can I do for you?"

From my purse, I take a Café Louis business check. "I need to settle the restaurant's account."

Joe frowns. "You're not going to order from the farm anymore?"

"No. I'm closing Café Louis."

Joe looks at me from under his baseball cap. He looks surprised, which I anticipated. He also looks sympathetic, which I didn't anticipate. I offer him a small smile.

"I'm sorry to hear that," he says. "Tough decision?"

"Yes. But it's what is best for my family."

Joe nods, then turns to a filing cabinet. He removes a stack of invoices, then punches numbers into a calculator. "Three hundred dollars and twenty-three cents."

"Okay. Do you have a pen?"

Joe gestures to a pile on his desk. I walk to the desk and take hold of a pen, then gesture to the chair opposite the desk. "Is it okay if I . . ."

"Sure." Joe watches me sit. I lean on the desk and fill out

the check. I'm close enough to smell Joe's sweat. Which means he can smell the perfume I just happen to be wearing.

"You could have done this over the phone," he says.

"Yes." I hand him the check. "But I came to apologize. My charming works better in person."

Joe smiles. "Thanks. For the check and the apology."

"I enjoyed spending time with you this summer," I say. "I liked talking to you. And singing with you. Dancing on the beach with you. And kissing you."

"You're right." Joe takes off his hat, and his hair falls into his face. "Your charming works well in person."

"Well, could I interest you in the other parts of my personality? Or did my cranky scare you off?"

"I thought I wasn't a man for all seasons."

"Farmer Joe, I'd like to see how you hold up in autumn."

"I think you'll find that I'm not perishable," Joe says.

"That's good." Should I . . .

Yes, says the diva.

I agree.

I stand and walk around Joe's desk. He looks up at me, and I lean forward. I kiss his mouth. The stubble of his beard grazes my cheek. It feels good. I stand straight.

"Was that okay?" I ask.

Joe frowns. Then he puts his hands on my hips and pulls me onto his lap. "This would work better." He kisses me. He tastes orange.

"Joe?"

"Yeah?"

"When was the last time you were in Europe?"

Melissa Jacobs

The Harder Choice

Bette meets me at Café Louis on the morning of the restaurant auction. I haven't seen her since I blew out of the restaurant after the Asbury Park incident.

"Thanks for coming," I say as I look at her. Bette looks the same as she always does, although her eyes are sad.

"I didn't think you'd want to watch the auction," she says.

"I don't," I say. "But I'd like to know where the pieces find homes. Maybe, one day, I can walk into a restaurant, look to an iced tea vat, and know that it was Dad's."

Bette smiles. "I guess he's really gone."

"Bette, is there anything you would like to take? As a memento? Anything you want. Just take it. Before the auction starts."

She looks around the restaurant and walks to the counter. Bette runs her hands along the counter. She looks at me. "I have my memories. That's enough."

And I have my memories.

"I've tried to do right by everyone who worked with us for so long," I say. "I don't have a pension to give you. But I think my father would want you to have something." Whatever Bette did or didn't do with my father, she has been loyal to Café Louis.

I reach into the pocket of my jeans and walk to the counter. "These are for you," I say. On the counter, I put the keys to Sally.

228

"She's your car," Bette says. "What will you drive?"

"I'm going away for a while," I say. "I won't need a car. When I get back, I'm going to buy my own car."

"But Sally was your father's," Bette says.

"And now, she's yours." I take the ownership papers from my purse. "Take care of Sally."

"Thank you," Bette says. She comes from around the counter, toward me. Bette smiles at me. Here she stands, this woman who has answers about my father. This is my chance to ask the question. It would be so easy.

But maybe the harder choice is not to ask. To let Bette leave with her dignity. Even the suggestion of an affair would insult her. Not that she would tell me the truth anyway.

If Bette's not going to tell me the truth, why should I ask? Why should I distort the memories I have of my father? Why should I insert the past into Mom's present?

Is it easier to live with the truth or without it? If I knew the truth, I wouldn't be able to un-know it. But living with my questions and uncertainties, for the greater good of my family? That is my choice.

And so, I say, "Goodbye, Bette. Be well."

⚬▬◀ *Lip Gloss*

"Your brows have grown nicely," Lisa tells me as I sit in her waxing chair at The Make-Up Bar. "They are balanced."

"Time heals all brows."

"I just got the new lipsticks for autumn," Lisa says. "Want to try a few?"

"I've had it with lipstick. Do you have any gloss?"

☛ Olga, the Diva, and Me, Part Two

It's about time, Olga says when I take her out of the closet. I've been in there too long.

Sorry, I say.

Where are we off to now? she asks.

It's a surprise, I tell Olga.

We're going to have a traveling companion, the diva says.

Oh? Our *bubbeleh* has been a busy girl?

It's about time, the diva says.

How long will we be traveling? Olga asks.

A month, I say.

And then what? Olga asks. Are we coming back here?

I don't know yet, I say.

After a month, I'll be worn out, Olga says.

Me, too, the diva says. I hope.

Ach, such a dirty mind, Olga says. So who is the mystery traveling companion?

☛ Home

"Welcome back." The customs agent smiles as she closes my blue passport.

Minutes later, a cab carries us away from the airport toward the heart of the city.

We'll be here for a week, then pick up and move to another city. A month is not the longest time I've been in Europe, but I think this trip will feel longer than any other. Why? Because now I know what's waiting for me at home.

The leaves will slowly change colors and the air will slowly chill. Allison's belly will grow, as will the pumpkins at Hunter Farm and the construction of the new SHRED shopping center on what was the site of Café Louis.

The twins will start kindergarten. Sarah will advance to third grade, and I'll be back in time for her birthday. Allison and Jeremy have already begun to look for a new house.

What will I do when I return? I don't know. And I think that's great.

For now, I will do my work, enjoy my traveling, and await visits from Joe and Aaron. Looking out the window, I say, "Isn't the city beautiful?"

"Hang on," Mom says. "I need to put on my lipstick."

Want More?

Turn the page to enter
Avon's Little Black Book—

the dish, the scoop and the
cherry on top from
MELISSA JACOBS

Confessions of a Jersey Girl

Hello. My name is Melissa and I'm a Jersey girl.
  Know what? You are, too.
  I'll explain.

What is a Jersey girl? There are songs, movies, and books de-
voted to us. What makes us extra special? First, let me tell
you my definition of a Jersey girl.
  You are a Jersey girl if you sing in the car with the windows rolled down and the music cranked. What kind of
music? Any kind. Okay, not classical. You can't sing along
with it. But, rock, hip-hop, rap, country, Broadway show
tunes—it's all good for car singing. Oh, and how about car
dancing? Bopping your head, waving your arms or some such
movement, and tapping your feet. Which is difficult if you are
driving. Almost impossible if you are driving stick shift. Still.
Car dancing is key.
  You are a Jersey girl if you own a thong. Or a lacy pair of
panties. But really, every woman should own a thong. Not
only to resolve panty line issues. Thongs make us feel sexy,
and just a little uncomfortable. Which is good. We shouldn't
be stuck in a panty rut, wearing the same old white cotton
undies day after day. What fun is that?
  You are a Jersey girl if you have a favorite scrunchie. Yes, I
know no one admits to wearing them anymore, but we all
have them tucked into bathroom drawers. There in that
drawer, hidden or not so hidden, is your favorite scrunchie.
It's stretched out and the fabric is torn, but you can't dispose

of it because it smells like the ocean, or maybe you were wearing it the night that boy kissed you. Scrunchie nostalgia? Yes!

You're a Jersey girl if you have comfort clothes. That T-shirt from an ex-boyfriend, an Egyptian cotton robe, the college sweatshirt, a baseball hat you've had since high school. When the world goes to pot, you reach for clothes that make you feel safe. And you reach for your girlfriends.

You're a Jersey girl if you have girlfriends and if you have . . . may I say it? A Council of Girlfriends! Yes, Jersey girls have everyday friends, special occasion friends, emergency friends, fun friends, and forever friends.

You're a Jersey girl if you've had your heart broken. By anyone. Your high school boyfriend, your husband, Justin Timberlake. It's heartbreak that lets us know that yes, we will survive. You may not give love a bad name, but you know that sometimes love is like bad medicine. You may not be a tramp, but you were born to run.

So, what is a Jersey girl? Being a Jersey girl is less about geography and more about attitude. Are you reading this in Baltimore? Chicago? Paris? Moscow? Sydney? No matter where you're from, there's a Jersey girl inside you. And there's one inside me, too. It took me almost a decade to realize that, and embrace my inner Jersey girl. Now? I am proud to say it.

My name is Melissa. And I am a Jersey girl.

Restaurant Confidential

Behind the Scenes of Philadelphia's Restaurant World

by Michael Klein and Melissa Jacobs

Michael Klein is a restaurant and news columnist ("Table Talk," "INQlings") for the *Philadelphia Inquirer* and has edited Zagat Restaurant Survey's Philadelphia edition since 1993. He is also an adjunct professor at Temple University's School of Journalism.

MJ: Here we are, at a coffee shop in Philadelphia. It's 9:30 A.M. I hope you don't expect me to be funny at this time of day. Can I order a latte with a shot of wit?

MK: I don't see that on the menu.

MJ: Let's get to the getting. Neither of us is a professional chef, yet we know a good deal about food. I learned about food by working with chefs and purveyors. Kevin Klause was my first chef. I worked in the business office of White Dog Café when he was the executive chef. French food I learned from Olivier De Saint Martin. Albie Buehrer at Indian Rock Produce taught me about fruits and vegetables. I learned about seafood from Sam D'Angelo at Samuels & Son.

MK: Did you have a Farmer Joe?

MJ: I wish I had Farmer Joe! But, no. He's completely fictional. And you, Mr. Mike? How did you learn about food and restaurants?

MK: My parents owned restaurants when I was a baby. Then, I worked in a restaurant when I was in high school. The restaurant life is not for me.

MJ: See, I go on for five minutes. You cut to the chase. What about the restaurant life made it unappealing to you?

MK: The hours and the lack of stability.

MJ: Which is what draws some people to it.

MK: Right. Which is also why I love the people in the restaurant business. It attracts all kinds of folks. Starry-eyed dreamers who want to entertain and play host. Hard-working immigrants who literally want to put food on their own table. College students who make a quick buck waiting tables or tending bar.

MJ: How did you learn about food?

MK: I don't know shiitake from enoki. I'm not a foodie.

MJ: But you do the Zagat guide. The restaurant Bible.

MK: That's compiling, not reviewing. My role is the business of the restaurants. In my "Table Talk" column, I write about which restaurants have opened, which have closed, what chef is working where. It's the scene, not the cuisine.

MJ: I'm not in the scene anymore, but I sure had fun in the 1990s when I was a restaurant PR babe. Let's give people an idea of what the Philadelphia restaurant scene was like then. It was fun. Exciting. There was a newness, an energy. Lots of drama.

MK: You are a novelist, aren't you? I'm a reporter. Here are the facts. Striped Bass opened in 1994 and is generally credited with starting Philadelphia's second restaurant renaissance. There was a lot going on then. The Pennsylvania Convention Center opened in 1994 and brought in a lot of business travelers and tourists. Ed Rendell became Philadelphia's mayor in 1992. He was—and is—as governor, a huge cheerleader of the city's restaurants. Also, the economy was about to recover from its recession. It was a "perfect storm," a confluence of events that was about to put Philadelphia on the national dining map.

MJ: And you were the reporter to cover that storm. To restaurant people, your column is the big score. Getting things in "Table Talk" is a major coup. Keeping things out of "Table Talk" is just as important.

MK: Did you keep things out of my column when you were a publicist?

MJ: You betcha. But let's go back to the fun stuff. When I was part of the restaurant scene, it was about vertical food, baby lettuces, Chilean sea bass, the birth of the Food Network and—

MK: Lots of hype. I really and truly think that the PR machines had a lot to do with the rise of restaurants here. PR people were feeding the public's need for celebrities. I mean, chefs as celebrities?

MJ: Well, let's talk about that. What defines a celebrity chef?

MK: How much he's paying a publicist.

MJ: That's not fair. There are of lots of great chefs who become known for . . . Okay. You're right. But in defense of my past self, and of publicists everywhere, we can't create nothin' from nothin'. A chef has to be a good chef in order for a publicist to turn him or her into a celebrity. Like Nick. His talent as a cook is not in question. So, do you have to have the raw ingredients to become a celebrity chef?

MK: Of course you need talent. But there are hundreds of talented chefs out there. Nick has Dine International, a big corporation, behind him. And a willing waitress in front of him.

MJ: "Sex, drugs, and linguine" is how Mimi describes the life of a celebrity chef. Is she right? Is being a celebrity chef like being a rock star?

MK: Most definitely. The bad hours, the high pay, the visibility—and there's that "bad boy" mystique. Girls go nuts over them. Too bad there are no print journalist groupies.

MJ: I'll be your groupie! But we can talk about that later. I can think of many Philadelphia restaurant stories which you broke. Scooped. Served up. Whatever. What are some of your most memorable?

MK: I'd have to say the departure of the opening chef of Striped Bass. She quit by leaving notes on her bosses' desks and flew to Vegas. She called me late that night from a hotel and told me what she had done. I had the story in Sunday's paper. The first time I made page one was when Georges Perrier of Le Bec-Fin almost chopped off four fingers in a food processor.

MJ: More, more!

MK: How about the drugged-up coowner of an Old City restaurant who left his wife and two very young children for a waitress?

MJ: Is that [name deleted]?

MK: No. It was [name deleted]. You're thinking of when [name deleted] left town with [name deleted].

MJ: Oh, right. Whatever happened to [name deleted]?

MK: Rehab.

MJ: And [name deleted]?

MK: Jail.

MJ: You know who I bumped into yesterday? [Name deleted.] She's still having an affair with [name deleted].

MK: She is? I didn't know that!

MJ: Oh, yeah. It's not an affair anymore because she divorced her husband. After the affair started.

MK: You're just telling me this now?

MJ: I know how to keep secrets.

MK: So do I. There are some things that I will take to my grave.

MJ: Let's move on. In the book, Madeline states that there is a difference between pastry chefs and "regular" chefs. Do you agree?

MK: Yes. Pastry chefs are almost always skinny. Wiry. With metabolisms like humming birds.

MJ: That's Madeline.

MK: I liked Madeline. Clever with the name. You're such a smart cookie.

MJ: Hardy har. Let's go beyond the chefs. What about the wait staff? How important are they to a restaurant? Like Bette and Christopher von Hecht.

MK: Wait staff can make or break a restaurant. To regular customers, a restaurant's wait staff becomes a family.

MJ: An incestuous family. It's the same in restaurants all

over the world. Even New Jersey. So, how is the Jersey dining scene different than the Philadelphia dining scene? As I wrote in the book, there is a preponderance of chain restaurants. Has that limited the growth of independent restaurants? Isn't it hard for independents to compete with national chains?

MK: There are chains everywhere. The problem in Jersey is that most of the residential areas are in developments near highways. That kind of commercial real estate is expensive and only chains can afford it.

MJ: Hence, the prosperity of Aaron Schein and SHRED. Did I realistically portray the plight of Café Louis versus SHRED?

MK: Yes. It's a scenario that is playing out every day. Unfortunately. And unfortunately, we have to go. Our parking meters are going to expire.

MJ: One last question. What's your favorite food?

MK: Peanut butter. You?

MJ: Reese's Peanut Butter Cups. Chee•tos. No, wait. Blueberries. My favorite food is the French salad with greens, lardons, and egg. What's that called?

MK: I have no idea. We have to leave.

MJ: I also love empanadas. Bing cherries. Steak frites. And moules frites. My mother's matzo balls. Silver Queen corn.

MK: I'm leaving.

MJ: Saga Bleu cheese. Linguine, of course. Churros. Gala apples. Sushi. Mike? Mike?

L3 Soundtrack

compiled by

Melissa Jacobs and Dave Jacobs

L3 is about family, right? So, I asked my brother to help me compile this soundtrack. We both love music. Dave has a great ear for matching music to moods. When I was a so-called student at the University of Pennsylvania, I was a DJ at Smokey Joe's, the best bar on campus. And on the planet.

What is this soundtrack for, exactly? Listen to it while you are reading the book. Better yet, listen to it during the summer. In your car. While car tripping. Driving down the shore (that's Jersey-speak for going to the beach) requires good, loud rock 'n' roll. On that, my brother and I agree.

And so, Dave and I present our favorite summer driving music. Beginning with Jersey's rocker laureate, Master Springsteen; moving through native faves the Bon Jovi boys to classics from the eighties; and including the Apostle Bowie, my patron saint.

"Thunder Road"
   (Bruce Springsteen, *Thunder Road*)
"Home"
   (Marc Broussard, *Carencro*)
"Ain't Even Done with the Night"
   (John Mellencamp, *Hurts So Good*)
"Jersey Girl"
   (Tom Waits, *Heartattack and Vine*)
"The Joker"
   (Steve Miller, *The Joker*)
"Wild Summer Nights"
   (John Cafferty, *Eddie & the Cruisers* movie soundtrack)

"And We Danced"
   (Hooters, *Nervous Night*)
"Captain Crash and the Beauty Queen from Mars"
   (Bon Jovi, *Crush*)
"Vertigo"
   (U2, *How to Dismantle an Atomic Bomb*)
"Young Americans"
   (David Bowie, *Young Americans*)
"Are You Gonna Be My Girl"
   (Jett, *Get Born*)
"Give It Away"
   (Red Hot Chili Peppers, *BloodSugarSexMagik*)
"Mr. Brownstone"
   (Guns 'N Roses, *Appetite for Destruction*)
"Smells Like Teen Spirit"
   (Nirvana, *Nevermind*)
"Plush"
   (Stone Temple Pilots, *Core*)
"American Woman"
   (Lenny Kravitz, *5*)
"Born to Run"
   (Bruce Springsteen, *Born to Run*)
"Alive"
   (Pearl Jam, *Ten*)
"Fall to Pieces"
   (Velvet Revolver, *Contraband*)
"Changes"
   (David Bowie, *Changes*)
"Freefallin' "
   (Tom Petty & the Heartbreakers, *Full Moon Fever*)
"Right Now"
   (Van Halen, *For Unlawful Carnal Knowledge*)
"I Try"
   (Macy Gray, *The ID*)
"Beautiful Girl"
   (Pete Droge and the Sinners, *Beautiful Girls* movie soundtrack)
"Freedom"
   (George Michael, *Listen Without Prejudice*)

"Run-Around"
  (Blues Traveler, *Four*)
"American Girl"
  (*Tom Petty & the Heartbreakers*)
"Bad Medicine"
  (Bon Jovi, *Slippery When Wet*)

MELISSA JACOBS

Christopher Williams

MELISSA JACOBS has spent half her life working in restaurants, bars, and bakeries. As a public relations consultant, she got a behind-the-scenes view of Philadelphia's restaurant world. "Working in restaurants isn't just a job. It's an adventure." Now the author of *Lexi James and the Council of Girlfriends* embraces her inner Jersey girl and continues pursuing her dream of becoming a novelist. Although some nights she still dreams of fly orders, turning deuces into four-tops, and getting twenty percent tips.

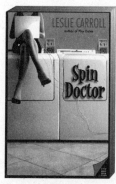